I CAN'T
GET NO
SATISFACTION

I CAN'T GET NO GET NO SATISFACTION

A
Swinging
Sixties
Mystery

Teresa Trent

First published by Level Best Books/Historia 2025

Author Photo Credit: MK Higginbotham

First edition

ISBN: 978-1-68512-870-8

Cover art by Level Best Designs

This book was professionally typeset on Reedsy.
Find out more at reedsy.com

Chapter One

March 1965

Can I see another's woe, and not be in sorrow too? Can I see another's grief,
and not seek for kind relief?
— *William Blake*

Mrs. Weaver sobbed quietly as I walked her and her husband back to Oliver's office. I didn't know what to say, and I had become pretty good at consoling the bereaved. This time, the circumstances were too much to soothe a troubled soul.

I had been working at the Fielding Funeral Home for over a month now, and I still couldn't get used to how sad some people were when they came in. Funeral directors had to work at becoming desensitized as they made their living around mourners who were suffering great losses. This couple lost their daughter in a senseless boating accident caused by a hit-and-run driver. She was only nineteen with so much of her life in front of her. Now, her parents were picking out her casket.

I needed this job and thought that helping people through this time would be something I could manage. I have always been a compassionate person, but this overwhelming grief broke my heart. After some mishaps at my last job, the town gossips labeled me "The Curse of Camden." With a name like that hanging over me, the phone wasn't exactly ringing off the hook, offering me secretarial jobs.

1

"Right this way, Mrs. Weaver." I opened a pristine white door and ushered the couple into my boss's office. Oliver Fielding was in his fifties, with gray hair and soft green eyes. Besides being a licensed mortician, he was also an experienced grief counselor and had a way of comforting even the most distraught clients. His patience and ability to wait on even the longest lapse into tears made him an excellent listener. Of all of my bosses I have to say I loved Oliver like a father. He was easy to talk to and always gave well-thought-out and reassuring answers. I knew the Weavers were well cared for.

"Thank you, Dot," Oliver said in the hushed tone he used around clients. It was as if we were always in a church where people were praying. I answered him in my own quiet voice, something I had cultivated since coming to Fielding Funeral Home.

"Certainly. Is there anything I can get you? Coffee or water?"

Mrs. Weaver looked down at her hands. She didn't answer, so Mr. Weaver said in a gruff voice, "No, thank you."

I took a chair across from them and picked up the steno pad I kept in Mr. Fielding's office. It would be my job to take down the parents' wishes for their daughter's funeral arrangements. As much as I hated taking dictation in secretarial school, in this job, it had come in handy. After Oliver finished the meeting with the Weavers, I would go back to my desk, type up the notes, and then put them in a fresh manila folder with their daughter's name on it.

"We are so sorry for your loss here at Fielding Funeral Home. So tragic, and your daughter was such a beautiful young woman, Oliver said. "I have a son her age and I can't imagine what you must be going through." His words were gentle, if not a little practiced. He always started a consultation with "We are so sorry for your loss here at Fielding Funeral Home," and then he added personal details from there.

"She loved animals, you know," Mrs. Weaver said. "She wanted to work with them after high school. Maybe work for a veterinarian. She actually went to the town council to ask if they would designate part of the park just for people to walk and play with their dogs. She wanted them to fence off the area so the dogs could run. You see, our dog Belle, a golden retriever, loves to run, but in the city, she can't run without getting in traffic. This would solve that problem."

Mr. Weaver looked out the window as he spoke. "She was so bright. She could have been an animal vet if she'd set her mind to it."

"Yes. Her boyfriend, Calvin, is going to college this fall, and we were sure he was going to ask her to marry him any day. We thought we'd have a summer wedding to plan for. Now, all of that is over. No wedding. No grandchildren. Just like that, life changes."

Listening to Mrs. Weaver, I realized that their daughter had been on the same path I was on. She had graduated from the same high school, wanted to find a fulfilling job, and her future life with her boyfriend was in front of her. She might have been a customer at my cousin's dress shop when she went to look for a wedding gown. I didn't remember her from high school, but I think we might have been friends if we had known each other.

"It sounds like she was a wonderful young lady." Oliver cleared his throat. "We received your daughter last night, and not to be indelicate, I would advise a closed casket."

After hearing this, Mrs. Weaver's quiet tears turned into sobs racking her body. Mr. Weaver put an arm around his wife, his own eyes filled to the brim of his lower lids. His cheeks and forehead flushed red. "You mean that S.O.B. hit her so hard we can't even look at our baby's face? If I ever find out who did this, I will personally see that their family is in this place arranging for a casket for them. How could something like this happen?"

Mr. Weaver's question was a common one. Even if people were expected to die, no one expected it. Dying happened to somebody else, not them. I paused over my steno pad, waiting for instructions from Oliver on the decisions Betty's parents were about to make.

"No one knows, sir. No one knows at all. If we did, we could stop a senseless accident like this from happening. From what the Camden Police Department has told me, they suspect there were drunk drivers out on the lake where your daughter was swimming near the shore. They had no business coming that close. You understand the boat did a lot of damage to her small body."

After sharing that horror about the condition of Betty Weaver's body, the only sounds in the office were the exhausted cries of the girl's mother. In my life so far, no one that close had died. I had a hard time understanding how Betty's mother could even sit there taking care of the business of burying her daughter. I would have trouble getting out of bed after such a loss. Still, she held it together enough to answer Oliver's questions.

We wrapped up the details for the Weaver funeral, and I escorted them back out. I returned to Oliver's office to pick up my notes. I found him looking out the window, his hand on his chin. "Have you seen Henry?"

It surprised me how we could go through a heartbreaking meeting like this and then revert to normal life in a flash. Oliver would acknowledge that what happened to the young girl was sad, but it was just another day at work for him.

"No. Didn't he go to put gas in the hearse?"

Oliver looked at his watch. "That was over two hours ago. Where can that boy be?"

The hearse was luxurious with leather padded seats and the paint shined so much you could see your reflection, but it wasn't exactly a car that would impress girls. No one thinks of a hearse when they picture their Romeo. "Maybe he had a flat?"

My efforts didn't comfort Oliver. He chewed on his bottom lip. "I think he would have called me. You know, he begged me to drive that hearse, and I was hesitant to let him do it because of his hearing loss. What if he doesn't hear a car horn beeping or an oncoming train? I want him to be a part of this business, but there are some things Henry shouldn't be doing. Driving is one of them."

"I'm sure he's fine." I gave Oliver a quick smile while hugging my notes from the meeting with the Weavers.

Oliver breathed through his nose, letting out a sigh. "I suppose you're right, but you have to understand that Henry's life has been a series of things that have been hard for him. The minute the kids at school found out Henry could only hear out of one ear, they teased him. Henry was so happy they were paying attention to him that he let them get away with it. Even though my only son is technically a man now, I still worry about people taking advantage of him."

I knew Henry in school, and Oliver was right. The boys picked on him. Henry was small in stature. He was at the mercy of some of the worst bullies at our high school. On top of his hearing loss, he wore glasses he often polished, and his speech was uneven. He looked like the ads in the back of magazines where muscular men kicked sand in the face of a scrawny guy on the beach. Oliver's worries were not unfounded and providing Henry with a safe job in a supportive family seemed ideal. Although I wasn't sure if Oliver knew it, sometimes his son wanted more than the life he had been given. He spent his downtime looking at magazines with muscle cars that sported voluptuous girls propped on the hoods. He started combing his hair back in the style of Frankie Avalon, making me hope there had to be an awkward, slightly shy Annette Funicello out there waiting for him.

His being overdue with the hearse was troublesome, especially because he was supposed to be waxing it before the next funeral. Oh, Henry, I thought. Where can you be?

"Where's Henry?" Neva Fielding came bustling in, a feather duster in her hand. Neva did afternoon dusting at precisely 2 p.m. This was the way she had always done it in the forty years she had spent working in the funeral home, first with her late husband and now with her son and grandson. Harley Fielding had built the funeral home when there was nothing else on Chestnut Street, a thoroughfare that ran through the main street of the town. Since that time, other businesses had been constructed and a nursing home was built across the street. No one was ever sure if they built there because they got a good price on the lot, or the proximity to the funeral home. As if the street were taking its cue from Fielding Funeral Home, two attorneys set up shop, as well as a home health agency. It was prime property, and if Oliver ever forgot that, his mother was there to remind him.

"We're not sure, Mother. He took the hearse out to get gas and hasn't returned yet." Oliver returned to his desk and started shuffling papers. He looked very busy suddenly, a sure defense from Neva's inquiries.

Neva delicately ran her fingers over the intricate lace of her high-necked cotton blouse, adjusting the collar to make it less stiff. "When did he leave?"

Oliver picked up a file from his desk, then looked up at me. "When would you say he left, Dot?"

Neva's eyes zoned in on me as she waited for my response.

"I'm not exactly sure, but it was after lunch."

Neva glanced at her wrist to check the time on her gold bracelet Timex watch. "Why, that's over two hours ago. Where is he?"

Neva posed a question that stumped both of us, resulting in neither of us providing an answer.

"I need to go type up these notes," I said softly, exiting out of the room as quickly as I could. As I padded across the deep maroon carpet to my sanctuary, Neva's voice echoed through the hall and into the lobby.

"Really, Oliver, you need to have a tighter rein over that boy. You're much too soft on him. Just because he can't hear out of one ear, that doesn't mean he can't follow instructions..." Neva often berated Oliver's parenting of Henry. Oliver, although he had to be irritated by his mother's constant scolding, remained a gentleman and promised his mother we would try to do better. Oliver might be the head mortician at Fielding Funeral Home, but Neva was the boss of the business and the family.

Henry showed up within the hour but quickly made himself scarce, saying he had other things to do. He dodged his grandmother by rushing to the basement before she could barrage him with questions. Oliver was busy working on Betty Weaver, so the mystery of those two hours would have to wait. After finishing my typing and filing, I filled a water can and watered the many potted plants in the funeral home. Neva detested droopy plants and listed the chore of keeping them upright in my job description. Oliver's father, who had passed ten years earlier, was the first Fielding to open the funeral home, and Neva made sure the standards were kept up. It wouldn't do for someone to come to a service to find their flowers wilting along with their loved one.

As I turned the corner, Ben walked in with mischief in his eyes. "Fancy seeing you here." He reached out and kissed me. Our engagement was a few months old, and we took every opportunity we could to be together. I wasn't sure how Neva would feel about seeing us in the clinch between the mums and gladiolas.

"Ben, don't do that. I'm at work. People are grieving."

He looked around the empty front lobby. "I don't see anybody, but let me ask you: do you see anyone? I mean, from the other side?"

"No, but Neva has been on the warpath about Henry, and she could walk in, or Oliver could come out of the embalming room."

He pulled me closer. "And that is when we'll stop kissing."

Even though I protested, I had to admit that his holding me close was a needed contrast to the sad meeting with Betty Weaver's parents. I realized I needed this little moment of joy.

After a minute, Ben pulled away. "So, I need to be honest with you because you're so hung up on this truth-telling thing. I'm here mostly on business."

I walked over to a wilting begonia, and picking up the can, added water. "What kind of business?"

"Betty Weaver. Have you seen her?" He looked around as if Betty were still able to make an appearance.

"No. I don't go down there, where they are working on the people."

Ben took out his trusty notepad. Even though he had offers for bigger jobs at newspapers in Dallas, he stayed back here with me in Camden. Someone from the big city might think he made a compromise for a slower life in a small town, but Camden had its share of murders.

"I guess your opinion on the body doesn't matter, seeing as you're not a mortician or medical expert, but have you heard anything more on the investigation? Have the parents been in? Did they talk about what happened to their daughter? Have the police told you anything new, like do they have a suspect?"

The can ran dry, so I set it down behind my desk. I turned around and straightened a series of brochures on the table. "I'm afraid I have to say no to all of that. All I've heard is that she was killed by a boater who was in the wrong part of the lake and that police are acknowledging several drunk people out that evening. I can also tell you that Oliver advised a closed casket."

Ben whistled through his teeth. "Man, that's terrible. Those poor parents. You know this had to happen with the way those kids are on the lake at night. It's like there's no law out there. Every boat has a six-pack and a stupid kid with a sunburn."

"You should have seen her mom and dad. Like they say, a parent shouldn't have to bury his child."

Ben put the notebook back in his pocket. He tipped his head toward me and leaned his forehead on mine. "If you hear anything, let me know."

I put my hands on my hips. "Ben Dalton. You know I'll never reveal anything I shouldn't. My job is to protect the family and respect the deceased."

"I know. I know. But someone in this town just got away with murder, and *The Camden Courier* will not let that person get away with it."

Chapter Two

We went to the county fair on Friday night, and though I had been to it all my life, this time there were a couple of things that were different. On this occasion, I was attending with my fiancée, Ben Dalton, and with my newly married cousin, Ellie, and her husband, Al. Even though we were legally adults according to our driver's licenses, we were searching for cotton candy and rides, just like any other kid strolling around the sawdust-covered fairgrounds. Rainbows of lights were spinning with every ride illuminating the sky. Children were everywhere, with sticky faces and pure joy in their eyes. Their laughter rang out from way above us as they floated up on the Ferris wheel. I took in the smell of popcorn and funnel cake and felt my heart lighten. One thing that differed from all my other visits to the fair was a recruitment table set up at the front of the fairway. Well-polished officers stood at the table with big smiles and exorbitant promises. The war in Vietnam had been going on for a little while, and from what I read in the newspaper, there was a push to enlist more and more boys to fight. Ben was just what they were looking for, and as we walked by the booth, I grabbed his hand to pull him away from the clutches of the smiling recruiters.

"Are you that eager to get on the Ferris wheel?" Ben asked.

I looked back at an Army recruiter who held a fresh form in his hand. "No, I'm just getting you away from the recruitment table."

"Oh, don't worry about me. Why would I ever want to leave my beautiful bride-to-be and Camden, Texas, the best little town in the West? I'll be right here with you working at *The Camden Courier* and loving every minute of it."

"What a relief." Everyone I know from high school joined up and never came back. Either they got killed or got a taste of life outside of our small town and decided rolling up the sidewalks at eight in the evening wasn't exciting enough for them.

"That's a definite promise, but I have to admit that it is pretty enticing for some of these guys."

"What guys?"

"Guys just out of high school, or guys who might be stumped about what to do to make a living. I decided I wanted to be a reporter when I was a teenager, but some people take a little longer to figure out what kind of job they want. I've had friends who went in and told me the Army, or whatever branch of the service, helped to instill discipline and give them a skill."

"Yeah, well, you can get that in prison, too."

"Miss Dot Morgan. That's very unpatriotic of you to say. We need men to go into service to protect our country. Did you forget about that?"

I felt silly now. "Yes. Absolutely. My dad and my aunt Mavis served in World War II and I don't know how my grandmother stood it. It's just the thought of losing you makes me crazy."

He looked into my eyes for a moment as if drinking me in and then kissed me, the rest of the world rotating around us in various states of joy.

"Don't you worry about that," he whispered. "If I go into battle, it will be with a press pass."

Mary Oliva, one of my dearest friends and the only woman on the Camden Police Force was also walking across the fairgrounds with her brood. Her husband John and the kids came up behind her, along with their abuela and her brother Carlos. She called out to me.

"Camden Police." She said in her official, slightly lower police voice. "Public displays of affection will not be tolerated, you two."

I laughed, especially when her husband John came up behind her, Marisol on his shoulders. "Yes, there are children present." Joey tugged on his arm, pulling him down the fairway, making Marisol tilt dangerously to one side. Ben stepped over to catch her if she fell, but John stopped and put her down. John's mother shook her finger at Joey.

10

"I'd better help John. He's got two wild kids on his hands. You two talk. Besides, Al and Ellie disappeared into the crowd. I'll find them. I'll meet you at the Ferris wheel," Ben said as he walked away.

We were standing by the carousel, and the sound of the music amplified as the horses spun around. I was glad to have a moment with Mary. "I haven't seen you in a while. Are things quiet down at the police department?"

When Mary didn't answer at first, I realized she was looking back at her brother Carlos, who was standing at the recruitment table. Carlos was twenty-one years old and had dropped out of school at sixteen. Since that time, he had worked a series of jobs, gotten married, and had a child. Mary had told me several times that she and John had loaned them money when they could, but without that high school diploma, Carlos was having a hard time meeting his monthly bills. He was exactly the kind of guy Ben had just been talking about.

Mary's eyes widened as he shook the recruiter's hand. "Oh no. I've got to stop him. They are trying to sign up soldiers for Viet Nam." She ran over to Carlos, who was now engaging in conversation with the Army recruiter. The recruiter pulled out a Zippo lighter and lit a cigarette while they were talking. Maybe Ben was right and young men doing their patriotic duty was a noble thing. I was all for it as long as I wasn't the wife waiting for her husband to do a tour in Vietnam. From the expression on Mary's face, she felt the same way.

I moved closer to Mary. "I thought you might need some help."

"Appreciated," she whispered.

The recruiter's towering voice was loud enough to hear clearly for several feet. He was an imposing man, and Carlos looked dwarfed beside him. We stepped closer to the recruitment table that was full of pamphlets and cards with Uncle Sam's picture on them. "Yes, sir, you can go into the Army, and you can make a steady salary and play catch up. Let me ask you, young man, did you finish high school?"

Carlos gazed at the ground. "No. Does that disqualify me?"

He took a quick drag of his cigarette. "Don't you worry about that. We have a new program we are instituting because we want to get this war over with. You know what I'm saying? We would like to make it easier for young men like you to enter the service and work on completing their schooling. We'll help you get your GED, and you can even put money toward college. By the time you get out of the service, you'll be on the right track for success in civilian life."

Mary stepped forward. "What about combat? Will this send him into the line of fire?"

The Army recruiter, who had been sailing along with his persuasive techniques with Carlos, turned around and frowned. "Don't you worry your pretty little head about that. Guns and fighting are men's business."

Mary pulled out her badge. "I'm a trained police officer, and I can tell you guns are my business, and I can also tell you that while you're promising all this catching up, you seem to be pretty slim on the details about the fact someone will be shooting at him."

"Excuse me, little Missy. I had no idea they had women on the police force these days. They let you carry a gun and everything." He laughed, and the Navy recruiter behind him laughed too.

It was like we were not people, invisible and too dumb to have a conversation about military service. I couldn't imagine what it would be like to be a woman in the military. Women were clearly pigeonholed into non-thinking roles. "I'll let you know that Mary is one of the best policewomen on the force. She saves people's lives."

"I think that's excellent. That's what her brother is going to do. Save the American way of life. You can't get any better than that, can you?" He turned his body to cut us off and grabbed Carlos by the shoulder. "Now, Carlos. May I call you Carlos?"

Carlos nodded.

"Excellent. What I need you to do is sign here so we can send it to headquarters to be processed. You should know that by signing up, you can pick up better assignments than if Uncle Sam starts up the draft again. Why not give yourself a little advantage over the rest of those slobs? Sound good?"

Carlos nodded eagerly. "You go on ahead, Mary. I'll catch up."

Mary stood there for a moment, but then finally turned and started walking. She put her hand on her head. "My brother does the stupidest things. He's been so worried about money, and now his wife is living with her mother. He's afraid he's losing everything, but this is not the answer."

From behind us, two guys I recognized from high school came by laughing. As they came closer, the Navy recruiter came forward, eyeing them like a shark seeing chum in the water. "Hello, fellas. Ever think about seeing the world?"

These two guys had been major bullies at our school and always seemed to have a joke between them that no one else shared. I remembered that the one with fair hair was named Chad. His dad owned Big Buck's Ford. His mother was one of the nicest people in Camden, and she served lunch in the cafeteria at the public school. "What are you crazy? Why would I want to join up? I have too much life to live, and all you swabbies want to do is take it away. Isn't that right, Jeff?"

"Damn straight." Jeff put his arm around Chad's shoulder and laughed. He was a few inches taller than Chad, but his physical size didn't mean he called the shots. Chad was clearly the ringleader in all their adventures and Jeff happily followed him.

"I wish my Carlos would listen to them," Mary said under her breath.

"No, sir," Chad said, "you're never going to get me over their slogging through the mud. That war is for some other sucker. Not me. So, tell me, is it true what they say about you sailors and long voyages out at sea?" Chad cocked his head to the side and gave the recruiter a mischievous wink, then he and Jeff walked off to the carnival runway, the laughter erupting again.

The sailor put his hands in his pockets and shrugged his shoulders. "Some guys think they're funny."

Carlos was busy signing the documents at the makeshift table. Mary quietly shook her head.

"He should have talked to his wife. He has a baby he needs to think of first. I know this is not going to work out."

I looked around the fairgrounds. It was a direct contrast to the gritty images I was seeing of Viet Nam on my black-and-white TV. "It seems like this war has crept up on us. I'm not even sure what we're fighting for."

"I don't know where Vietnam is on the map," Mary said, her eyes on her brother. " I'm sorry for whatever is happening over there, but right now, I'm fighting for my family."

"I'm sure it will be okay," I said to Mary, who crossed her arms and shivered, even though the temperature was a little stuffy on the fairgrounds.

"Sure. I'm going to try not to think about it and enjoy this evening with my family."

"Right, this only happens once a year; let's enjoy tonight." I could see Ben up ahead, standing by the Ferris wheel. "There's Ben. I think he wants to kiss me on top of the Ferris wheel."

Mary smiled. "Yes, I think you're right. I think he wants to kiss you on every single ride he can get you on."

Henry Fielding stepped in front of us and approached two young, attractive girls who were getting cotton candy. Henry's bony chest was prominent through the maroon and white striped short-sleeved turtleneck. He took out a cigarette and then pulled out a red, white, and blue matchbook. I had never seen Henry smoke before. I wondered if Oliver knew his son had taken up smoking? He lit the cigarette and gave a devil-may-care smile to the girls. "Good evening, ladies. Would any of you like to go on a ride with me? I'm paying."

Behind Henry, his friend Nelson stood off in the distance, his arms crossed as he leaned against the garish paint of red, orange, and green of the wall of the funhouse. His little brother, Arnie, tugged at his arm, trying to pull him down the midway, but he brushed him away as he watched Henry. Nelson visited the funeral home almost daily and didn't mind chatting with Henry, even if he was occupied in the embalming room. Oliver said the two had been close friends since middle school. Nelson's face showed signs of rampant acne in his younger years, and his nose was a little large for his face. It was strange that he was hanging back the way he was. The two friends were usually inseparable. Had they fought? Nelson did not look happy. Hopefully, he was playing wingman to Henry's romantic approaches.

The girls giggled behind their hands. "No, thank you." They answered in a

14

chorus.

"You're missing out."

They started to walk away. "No, we're not."

Henry pulled his hands out of his pockets, placed them both in the air, and shrugged. "Your loss."

Nelson had witnessed the entire scene and sneered at Henry, then Arnie won the battle and propelled him down the midway to the rides.

I had worked side by side with Henry and had never seen this side of him. It was like his mousey existence had transformed him into a wolf. We worked with clients, but rarely with attractive young ones. Maybe this was a Henry I didn't know about.

"Hey Henry, how are you?" I asked, wondering if he would return to his quiet demeanor when he saw me.

He turned. "Dot!" He acted as if we hadn't seen each other every day that week. "Marvelous to see you, my dear." His glance landed on Mary. "And who is this?"

"Sorry, this is my friend and one of Camden's finest, Mary Oliva."

"Finest what?" He cocked his head to the side, looking confused, merriment in his eyes.

"The finest policewoman. Mary's a cop."

His smile faded. "Oh. Nice to meet you."

"Nice to meet you as well. Dot has told me so much about working with you and your dad. I don't know how you do what you do."

Henry nodded. "I could say the same of your job."

Being at the fair had made Henry fairly chatty, so I asked him what I'd been wanting to know since he disappeared with the hearse. "Say, I have a question for you. You never told us where you went with the hearse for two hours."

"Oh, that!" He put his fingers on his chin and smiled. "A man can't tell all of his secrets now, can he? Let's just say things are turning around for Oliver Fielding's mortician's assistant."

There was something about him that was different. I couldn't quite put my finger on it, but he was more worldly, or at least acting that way. I pushed him a little further, something I had never done before, mostly because it never seemed he had a secret before. Whatever was going on with him, I wanted to know. "Really? How?"

Henry smiled and leaned forward. "Like I said, things are good, and right now, all I want to do is enjoy my night at the fair. I need to catch up with some friends. See you tomorrow, Dot."

That was curious because the only friend Henry had was in the other direction. As Henry walked away, Mary pulled me closer. "He's pretty full of himself. He also isn't comfortable around me being a cop. I only get that kind of reaction when someone has something to hide."

As I watched Henry walk away, there was a little lilt in his step. Something about him had changed, and it had something to do with his two hours away from the funeral home. "I wish I knew what he's hiding. Henry is normally quite meek and mild. This is a new guy. I wonder what's changed."

Before he could get too far, his friend Nelson caught up with him. He pulled on Henry's arm to get his attention, but Henry pulled away. It was obvious; even from a distance, he was brushing his old friend off. Whoever Henry was rushing to meet, it hadn't been Nelson, and his one genuine friend wasn't taking it well.

"What is going on with you?" Nelson yelled loud enough for us to hear.

Henry said something in a softer voice and then walked away, leaving Nelson standing alone on the carnival walkway. The Navy recruiter, seeing Nelson, approached him and flashed a pamphlet, but he pushed the man away, nearly knocking him over. Nelson's face was an angry red. He walked off, the remaining recruiters staying where they were, wise enough when to shy away from a war front.

Mary shook her head after witnessing the scene. "I wish my Carlos would have done that." She glanced over at her brother, who was now in a deep conversation with the slick recruiter. "I need to go catch up with John. The kids are driving him crazy by now. That Henry is one interesting guy. I'll say one thing for you, Dot. You never seem to have a boring job."

She was right. Even working in the somber surroundings of a funeral home, unexplained things were going on. Not with the dead, but with the living. Henry had a secret and whatever it was had changed him. After seeing him rebuff his closest friend, I wasn't sure if it was a change for good or for bad.

Chapter Three

On the day of Betty Weaver's visitation, the funeral home was filled with Betty's friends, neighbors, and family. Oliver was in his element, going from group to group, while I was making sure that everyone's needs were met while listening for the phone. Upon Oliver's advice, Betty's parents had opted for the closed casket, and the mourners quietly walked up to pay their respects. The room was lined on every wall with bouquets, some in pots, while others were displayed on green metallic stands. It was hard to take a breath without feeling the floral aroma nest in your nostrils. I loved the smell of flowers, but when they were bunched together in the stuffy visitation room, it was cloying.

Oliver's mother, Neva, was buzzing around in her black crepe dress with two strings of pearls accenting her double chin. I stood near the wall, watching the scene, when Neva nudged me. "Make sure the visitation line is moving, dear. It's very hard for some of these people to wait for their last few minutes with their beloved."

I liked Neva. She was bossy, yes, but she had been in the funeral business for most of her life and went out of her way to make it a comfortable experience for the mourners. She straightened the hymnals in the pews of our tiny sanctuary. She felt the leaves of the plants to make sure they weren't drying out. She made sure there wasn't an inch of dust in the entire funeral home and that Henry and Oliver always looked highly professional with straight ties and combed hair. It was her little touches that caused families to come back to the funeral home for all of their funeral needs, over and over again. I didn't know anyone in Camden who had not attended a funeral at Fielding's.

No one even considered going out of town to have their loved one buried.

Henry was in his own little world, working in the back and coming into the visitation room here and there. He was in an excellent mood, which was unusual for him. He was usually quiet and stayed to himself. But today he was acting differently. He was smiling. And it wasn't the gentle, caring undertaker smile of his father, but more like a smile, you would see on the face of someone who has just won a prize. Maybe he finally got a girl to go up on the Ferris wheel with him, and for his sake, I hoped that had happened.

His friend, Nelson, was just the opposite. He sulked as he held a teacup and leaned against the wall, his eyes always on Henry. Whatever was going on between them was still there. Nelson's mother, Dina, had also been circulating, but mostly keeping Nelson's brother Arnie out of the food that had been prepared by the friends and family of Betty Weaver. Arnie reached for a small cupcake and spilled crumbs on the floor. Oliver walked over and handed Arnie a napkin to put underneath it. Dina gave Oliver a grateful smile. As she passed Nelson, she said something in his ear, resulting in him standing up straight. He didn't look any happier, but he stopped leaning. Dina lost her husband in an oil refinery accident five years earlier in South Houston. He was a volunteer fireman and lost his life while trying to rescue another man. When a tank exploded, they both perished. When Nelson's father died, Dina moved up to Camden, where her parents were. She had never remarried, spending most of her time raising her sons and working as a receptionist at a local veterinary clinic.

Dina came by the funeral home occasionally to pick up Nelson, and because Nelson and Henry were friends, so were Oliver and Dina. I always wondered if there were more between them, but Oliver could be quite reserved if he wanted to be. Dina glanced at Henry, who was avoiding Nelson, and then at Oliver, who was also observing the rift between the two boys.

At times, I would see mourners whispering to each other behind cupped hands. They couldn't help it. The mystery was too tantalizing not to talk about. Betty Weaver's death was being investigated as an accident, and the driver of the unknown boat was still at large. I had to wonder if they were all thinking what I was thinking. Could the killer be among us today?

Margaret Doggett stood near the back and looked different without the hairnet she wore while serving lunch to Camden's children. Today she wore a dark floral dress, but instead of heels, she had on the comfortable shoes I'd seen her wear in the lunchroom. Her short hair was heavily sprayed and moved in one piece when she turned her head. Many of the students who were there for Betty also came up and spoke to her. She never taught a single class, but everybody knew the lunchroom ladies, and Margaret was known to put a little extra dessert on the plate. She clutched her white handbag to her middle and lit up every time one of her "kids" would come by to say hello. It was said that one of the school's favorite dishes, "the brownie surprise," was Margaret's recipe. She was deeply loved by the community, and, of course, she would take time to visit Betty Weaver and her family.

Someone had left a teacup on a table, and I went over to pick it up. The two guys from high school I had seen at the fair, Chad and Jeff, leaned up against the wall, whispering as they viewed the assembled crowd. They had been a couple of years younger than me in high school, and since seeing them at the fair, my memory of what they were like was coming back to me. They were always up to something. I only hoped that wouldn't include something at Betty Weaver's visitation. There was an empty cup sitting next to Jeff, and I knew that if Neva saw it, she would rush over to get it. "Excuse me," I said as I stepped around them to get the cup.

"Dot? Dot Morgan? The prettiest senior girl at Camden High?" said the taller boy, with dark brown hair and a face that could land him a job in Hollywood. He was a handsome kid, but he didn't seem to be interested in capitalizing on his good looks.

"I don't know about that. You're Jeff, right?" I asked.

"Jeff Hudson. You were a senior when we were sophomores. Oh my, Miss Dot Morgan. Cheerleader, Prom Queen, you were everything a young boy desired."

The way he said "desired" embarrassed me, like I was the girl with the staples in her navel in Playboy. I felt the heat rise to my cheeks. Before I could say anything, the other young man stepped up. "And I am Chad Doggett. I asked you to dance at homecoming, and you lowered yourself to dance with a sophomore."

"Yeah, but then she went back to her date. Who was that anyway?" Jeff said.

"Uh, Tim, I think," I said. "I'm not quite sure where he is today." I also didn't remember dancing with Chad, but I chose not to share that part.

Chad raised his eyebrows, merriment in his eyes. "He left a lasting impression on you, did he?"

"I guess not," I said. "So, were you friends with Betty?"

Chad glanced at the closed coffin and nodded. "Yeah. We dated a couple of times. I eventually figured out she wasn't for me."

Jeff rolled his eyes. "As usual. Chad here, can't seem to settle on one girl. One day he'll be a lonely old bachelor with only me to play chess with in the park."

Chad punched Jeff's shoulder, and from the sound of the soft thud, it was going to leave a mark. "Shut up. You're so stupid you didn't even figure out you'll be old and lonely, too."

"I didn't say that. My wife would be at home being wifely. I'd just come out to keep you company, old man." Jeff said, now holding his arm.

Feeling the need to move on, I changed the subject. "I haven't seen you since high school. What are you doing now?"

"As little as possible," Chad said. Jeff laughed.

It was like being on a game show where the host made a wisecrack about everything. I liked a joke as much as the next person, but with these two, it made me uncomfortable. "You must be wealthy, then?"

Jeff gave me a wink. "Oh, don't worry about Chad here. His mom is the sweet old lunchroom lady. She'd like him to stay home for the rest of his life. I wish my mom and dad were like that. Then he also has his dad, Big Buck Doggett, of Big Buck's Ford." He said the last part like a full-throated radio announcer.

"And what about you?" I asked.

"Me? I'm selling vacuums door to door. My mom got me the job, and I hate it, but she's all hung up on men making a living after my father packed his bags. Just between you and me, he did us all a favor, but here." He reached for his wallet, pulled out a card, and handed it to me. On it was *Jeff Hudson, Home Cleaning Specialist. Call for a demonstration of our latest model.*

"So why don't you go to college?" I asked.

Jeff snorted and then laughed a little too loudly for a visitation. "No, thank you. I've had enough of school. The only reason I'd go to college would be for the parties."

"Amen, brother," Chad added, putting his hands in prayer formation.

Jeff put an arm around Chad. "And brothers we are. Two men, alone, against the world."

If they kept this up, I thought the sound of a whistling war theme would start to ring throughout the reception. They were like John Wayne and Steve McQueen marching off to battle. I thought about the direction my parents steered me into, going to secretarial school. What would I have done if I had a college degree? I always wanted to go, although I had no idea what kind of major I would study. Now it seemed too late. It also made me a little angry that these two boys might have had that choice on the table and chose not to pursue it. These two were working so hard to have a good time that it was kind of sad.

Margaret Doggett left her seat and came over. "I see you met my son and his friend."

"Mrs. Doggett, it's so nice to see you." I hugged her. "They were telling me about what they were planning for their futures. Live every day to have fun, seems to be the general idea. "

Margaret puckered her top lip in a frown. "Can you blame them? His father wants both of his sons to join the Army, and Chad has promised he will. My son, Steve, has already joined, and as a mother, I find it all terrifying. What if something were to happen to him?"

My thoughts flashed back to Mary and her concern for her brother Carlos getting himself in the line of fire.

Margaret continued talking. "My Buck was a WWII hero, but he isn't the same man who left here. These young men need to enjoy their lives."

Both Jeff and Chad nodded their heads in agreement. They liked what she was saying.

Chad smiled. "Don't worry, Mama. We plan to enjoy every minute."

Margaret put her hand on the collar of her floral dress. "From your lips to God's ears." She then looked across the room. "Oh, the parents have a minute. Let me go express my condolences. Chad, would you like to go with me?"

Chad shifted. "No. I think I'll skip it. Her old man never liked me."

"Fine." Margaret turned to me. "Good to see you, dear." Chad's mother toddled over to Mr. and Mrs. Weaver, who looked even more tired than the day they had visited Oliver to plan the funeral. After all of this was over, they would return home to a quiet house. It was a direct contrast to all the people milling about here, and the thought of it made me feel sad for them. Their Betty would never be there again. No June wedding. No grandchildren.

Henry joined us. He smiled broadly at Chad and Jeff. "Hi, guys. I'm glad you made it. Can I get you two gentlemen anything?" I couldn't get over how nice Henry was being, and he was still flashing that smile. It was like they had never bullied him when he was younger. I knew people changed once they left the halls of high school and became nicer people, but it hadn't been that long, and from my observations, these two hadn't changed. Yet here was Henry, acting like an old pal of theirs.

Chad raised his eyebrows in a conspiratorial fashion. "You got any booze in this place?

Henry stammered, some of his confidence slipping. "No. Uh, we have tea or coffee."

Jeff moved closer. "Come on, Henry. There must be something in this place other than embalming fluid." Henry's bottom lip quivered. Chad reinforced his push by putting an arm around Henry's shoulders. From my conversations with Henry and our years in school together, I never remembered them being friends. Chad and Jeff bullied Henry. What had changed?

"We're friends, right? Your old man has to have something stashed somewhere." Chad suggested.

That buoyed Henry's confidence some, and he put on a face I hadn't seen before. Now he was trying to be the 98-pound tough guy. He had all the bravado of Barney Fife, flashing the only bullet he was allowed for his gun. "You know how it is. The old man has a hard-ass rule about drinking at funerals."

Chad's mouth curled into a scowl. "What a shame. I guess that will shorten our little visit. I never liked this chick, anyway."

Jeff nodded, modeling the same expression. I hoped Betty's parents hadn't heard the callousness of these so-called mourners. It was easy to see why she and Chad only dated a few times.

Chad walked over to his mother. "We're going."

She turned. "So soon? I was about to speak to Betty's mother and father."

Chad looked exasperated. "Maybe you shouldn't have wasted so much time sitting here."

Chad took his mother's arm and led her out, with Jeff following.

Oliver came over and stood next to me and Henry, his eyes focused on Chad and Jeff. "What was that all about?"

"They had another appointment," Henry said a little too quickly.

"They asked whether we were serving alcohol," I added.

"Alcohol? Really? Those boys are Henry's age, and it is only one in the afternoon. Who drinks that early in the day?"

I agreed, but Henry looked at his shoes. Oliver said in a low voice, "As soon as the reception is over, we'll need to clean up this room to get it ready for the Hanssen funeral tomorrow."

From the expression on Henry's face, he didn't like that idea at all. "Can't we do it in the morning? I have plans tonight." As Henry pleaded with his father, his voice level rose.

"Shhh," Oliver said, while glancing around the room.

"What kind of plans?" I whispered, nudging him with an elbow. "You have a hot date or something?"

Henry blushed. All the time I had been working here, I'd never seen Henry with a girl. So, if that was the case, it was big news.

"It's… It's personal," Henry stuttered.

"Well, whatever it is, we need to prepare this room first." Oliver left us and moved on to check on Betty Weaver's parents.

"I'll help you," I whispered.

"Thanks, Dot."

Nelson had been watching the entire scene, but when my gaze caught him staring at us, he turned away. He looked more than hurt. He looked angry.

Chapter Four

That evening, Ben and I had been invited to Ellie and Al's home for dinner. They had been married for four months, and Ellie was trying to do wifely things like entertain with panache. She had been reading *McCall's Ladies Magazine* and wanted to set the mood for the perfect dinner party.

Ellie wore a blue floral dress with a delicate white apron at her waist. She was the embodiment of the Betty Crocker face I'd seen in her cookbook. Her hair was a little more teased than she normally wore it, and I couldn't help but notice there were circles under her eyes. Maybe working full-time to run a successful dress shop and then rushing home to cook a magazine-worthy dinner was exhausting her.

Ellie handed me a set of cloth napkins, and I sat them on each plate.

"It looks wonderful, Ellie," I said, noticing the ironed white tablecloth and the flowers set just so in the center of the table.

"Thank you. I've been marinating the meat all day." She let out a tired sigh.

"Are you feeling okay? You look a bit peeked."

Ellie gave a quick smile. "I'm fine. You're only thinking I look unhealthy because you're spending too much time with dead people."

Al and Ben joined us in the dining room after having a heated discussion about the ball game playing on the television in the next room.

"Funny," Ben said as he stole a roll from the breadbasket, "but I know whose job you're talking about."

"You amaze me, Dot," Al said, taking a seat. "How can you stand to be around funerals day after day? The flowers alone would have me sneezing, and then there's so many sad folks milling around."

I shrugged. I was learning this was a pretty common question for people who worked in funeral homes. "I don't know. It's a job pretty well like any other, and Oliver is a great boss."

Ellie placed a platter of pork chops smothered in mushroom gravy on the table. "Your luck with bad bosses is worthy of Ripley's Believe It or Not."

I tried not to think about the truth in her statement and began to fill my plate. "Yeah, but not this time. Oliver is patient. Oliver is kind."

"Wait a minute. I think you're quoting scripture. He can't be that impressive," Ben said, then turned to Al. "You know they're calling Dot the 'Camden Curse' with all the murders she's found herself involved with."

"Stop," I said. I hated that name and didn't want that clever alliteration to spread.

"I heard it, too," Ellie added. "Admit it. The funeral home was the only place that would take you, probably because their clientele is already dead."

Everyone else at the table laughed, but I cut them short. "Okay, it's not the job I dreamed of when I was in secretarial school, but having a peaceful workplace has become very important to me."

Al snickered. "I'll say it's peaceful."

"These potatoes look delicious," Ben said as he put a scoop on his plate. He spooned up a mouthful and then, after a few chews, took a hard swallow.

I took a bite of mine, and my teeth hit a large, undercooked chunk. I tried to work it around my mouth, but it formed a bulge in one cheek. Ben saw it, and merriment twinkled in his eyes as he attempted to hold back a laugh.

"Yum," I said through my teeth.

Ellie, who had always been the brighter one out of the two of us, stabbed at her potatoes with a fork. "Damn. The cookbook said they would be soft and fluffy and melt in your mouth."

I took a sip of water, hoping it would help ease the lump in my throat. "I think Betty Crocker snuck too much cooking wine that day."

Ben and Al laughed, but Ellie rose from the table, threw down her napkin, and bolted for the door. I started to get up, but Al stopped me.

"I'll talk to her. She's been doing this a lot lately." Al rose and followed his new wife to the kitchen.

Ben's gaze followed Al. "Wow. What's going on with your cousin?"

"If I had to guess, I would say she's trying to do too much. It's asking a lot to work all day and then run a home like Donna Reed." I set down my fork. I was worried for my cousin. She was always the one who wanted to make everything perfect. That was why she was such a talented seamstress, and why her wedding dresses were in such high demand.

"Who is Donna Reed again?" Ben asked. I struggled to believe we grew up in the same country, and he didn't know about the family-centered program where everything always worked out before the end of the episode. If only real life were that easy.

"That woman who always wears pearls and keeps the perfect home. Where have you been, Ben Dalton? Didn't your parents let you watch TV?".

"And that's entertainment? I prefer the news," Ben said. He read more than he watched TV. Living with Ellie and her habit of turning on the set while she sewed, I saw all the shows on the three networks: ABC, CBS, and NBC.

I pushed my plate back, even though I was still hungry. I was grateful for the reprieve of having to pretend I could eat Ellie's dinner. "Any news on the Betty Weaver case?" I asked.

"A little," Ben said. "I have a hunch. How many people could there have been out on the lake that night?"

This was an interesting question. Betty Weaver was out swimming with friends on Thursday night because they wanted to swim but did not want to miss a dance on Friday. Thursday was not a big night on the lake.

"You've got a point. Is there any way of tracking what boats were out on the water?"

Before he could answer, Al and Ellie came back from the kitchen. Ellie's eyes were red, but she put on a brave face.

"Sorry about that, folks. My emotions got away with me." Ellie pulled out her chair and sat. Once there, she pushed her potatoes to the side of her plate. Her eyes were red and there was a little shake in her hand. She glanced at my and Ben's plates. "Oh no. Neither of you is eating. Is it that bad?"

Afraid I would send her into another spiral, I answered, "No! We were talking. That's all." I pulled my plate back to its former place and shoveled a spoonful of corn into my mouth while Ben sawed off a piece of meat.

"See there, honey. Everyone loves your dinner," Al said as he stroked her back.

Ellie sniffed and nodded to Al. They were so sweet together. It always amazed me that they waited as long as they did to get married. I felt bad that she looked so defeated.

"Ellie, just because you're married doesn't mean you have to be perfect."

"But I do. All the magazines, the shows we see on TV..."

"Is made up. Fake. Women today are different. They work outside of the home, so why should they be expected to keep a house worthy of a White House tour?"

"Oh, Jackie's tour was amazing." She was referring to the tour Jackie Kennedy did from the White House. It was wonderful, but she hadn't picked up a feather duster once to make it look that good.

"Yes, Jackie is amazing, but so are you. You run a business, and I'll bet you equal Al in take-home pay."

"She does." Al nodded.

"So relax a little. Will you? I've never seen you look so tired trying to do it all."

"Okay." She looked down at her hands, "I was dreading trying to pull off this dinner."

"When the diner is just as good, honey," Al said, and then, from the look in Ellie's eyes, double backed. "Not as good as this fine homecooked meal, though. What a treat."

"Thank you." She then shifted her focus to me, a little spark coming into her eyes. "Okay. That's over. I'm fine now. So, tell me about you, Dot. I expect you were talking about the wedding. Have you set a date yet?"

Oh, to have a nickel every time I was asked that question. My mother, her mother, the grocer, the baker, the candlestick maker. Ben put his warm hand over mine.

"Not yet," he said.

"Don't dawdle too long. I have so many ideas for your dress. How about a May wedding? You'll get a jump on the June brides," Ellie suggested, the light coming back into her eyes.

Ben pressed his lips together in thought and then asked me, "May? What do you think, Dot?"

It was one thing to say we were engaged, but quite another to be setting dates. I panicked and changed the subject. "We were talking about Betty Weaver's hit-and-run. Do you know anyone who owns a boat?"

With my quick departure on the subject of date setting, my dinner companions looked stunned.

After an uncomfortable few seconds, Al spoke up. "Bubba Jenkins has a boat. Keeps it at the marina. He always complains about how much he has to pay to keep it there."

"I think we might need to talk to him sometime, don't you, Ben?" I asked.

Ben rested his chin and his hand as he considered my idea. "I think we should, but first, I want to walk around the marina. Who knows what we might find?"

On Sunday, Ben and I decided to ask the marina owner, Shep Olmstead, if he had any records of the boats going out.

"A record of who takes boats out? Not really. The only records I keep are whether people have paid their boat slip rent," Shep said as he swept the dock, his trusty Australian shepherd, Selma, by his side. He wore the only outfit I had ever seen him in. A knit polo shirt and khaki shorts. My mother said he had been quite the catch in his day, but now he seemed to be content to run the marina with his trusty companion.

I patted Selma's soft brown and black fur. "Would you have any idea who might have been on the water the day Betty Weaver was hit?"

"Now that's a humdinger of a mystery. The police asked me the same question. The answer is no one. Before I go to bed each night, Selma and I walk the dock just to make sure everything is in its place. I have twelve boat slips, and twelve boats were all tucked up right nice."

Ben scratched his head. "What time was that?"

Shep leaned on the broom. "Oh, round about 8 p.m., I'd say."

"And you didn't hear anything during the night?" I asked.

"Not a thing." He shook his head to emphasize this point. "The next morning, twelve boats in twelve slips. Nothing had changed. It's an awful shame about that young lady."

Ben furtively glanced at the boats moored to the dock. The sun cast a golden glow on the water, while birds swooped overhead, their cries echoing through the air. The scent of diesel fuel mingled with the invigorating aroma of fresh lake water. The boat ramp was next to the marina where the twelve boats sat. "Could someone have launched a boat during the night?"

"It's a possibility," Shep answered, "but I think I'd hear the car or truck engine. Selma doesn't always bark at people, but she would have barked at something like that. Plus, whoever was unloading a boat would have left fresh tracks. The police didn't see any."

"Whoever it was, they must have been invisible. No one saw them, and no one heard them," Ben said.

"At least we don't think anyone saw them," I added. It was a beautiful afternoon with a slight breeze. Three of the boats were out of their slips. "It looks like your boaters are enjoying a day on the water."

"Yup. The Johnsons and Lennons both went out at about ten this morning. I'm not sure when Bubba Jenkins's boat went out. It was gone when I got up. Some people like to fish at dawn."

So, even though he wasn't saying it, he knew what was going on at his marina. "I guess even though you don't record anything on paper, you keep track of who has boats out," I said.

"I try," Shep answered.

We all turned at the sound of an approaching vehicle. A black and white Ford Galaxy pulled up, and two policemen exited in a hurry. The fact that the police were rushing to the marina made me think of Betty Weaver's death.

"Hey, Shep," a young patrolman tipped his hat. He took a notepad out of his pocket. "We're looking for the owner of a red Runabout. Do you have anyone with that kind of boat who rents space at the marina?"

Shep set down his broom. "Sure do. That would be Bubba's boat. You know, Bubba Jenkins. Not here now, though."

"I'm aware," the officer said. "I didn't know Bubba even had a boat."

Shep put his hand on his belt loop. "Well, it wasn't his to begin with. It's his inheritance. What's all this about, Officer?"

"Yes," Ben echoed. "What's this about?"

The marina became very quiet as we all waited for the answer. Whatever had happened, it sounded like it involved a boat. This was starting to feel like Betty Weaver all over again.

The young officer cleared his throat and bobbed slightly on his heels. "We found the boat at a crime scene just up a ways on the lake."

It was a pleasant Sunday afternoon. The last thing I would expect on a day like today would be any kind of criminal activity. "What happened?" I asked.

"We got ourselves another hit-and-run, but this time the driver left the boat along with the body."

Ben stepped closer to the officer. As he did, the accompanying officer also stepped forward. "And that would be Bubba Jenkins's boat? The red Runabout?" Ben lowered his voice. "*Camden Courier.* Do you have an identification on the body?"

The officer's eyes hardened. I remembered the many times Mary told me the officers of the Camden Police Department were warned of repercussions if they talked to the press. "We do, but we will not be releasing that information until we notify the next of kin."

Shep turned toward the marina office. "Let me get you that information on Bubba."

"This is big news," Ben whispered in my ear as Shep and the officer walked away. The radio in the patrol car began squawking about rescue vehicles, and the other officer returned to the police car. Ben put his arm around my waist and gave me an excited squeeze. "The case is afoot, Watson."

"And we're right in the middle of all of it." I took a breath and watched Shep and the officer talking through the window of the marina office. Two hit-and-run boating deaths in one town in one month. What were the chances?

Ben was pulling his keys out of his pockets. "First, let's go see if we can find the abandoned boat. This is big. We have a serial murderer whose weapon of choice is a boat. What a headline it will make."

Chapter Five

I hung my head out the window, searching for an opening through the trees. "This is an enormous lake. It could be anywhere." The trees and underbrush were thick in some places, making the lake disappear temporarily. The road meandered along the lake, though not precisely. Sometimes, it seemed to veer away from the lake completely.

"Look for flashing lights," Ben said, his eyes never leaving the road.

"I wonder if Mary has been called to the scene to assist."

"We can only hope. She'll tell us what's going on and who the victim is. You know we get those crazy boaters from Dallas. If it is, as sad as it sounds, that would be a good thing for me and mean I have a story that would potentially be picked up by the Dallas papers."

Even though Ben had turned down a position with the Dallas Morning News last year, he was a proponent of the "bloom where you're planted" way of thinking. Several of his stories had been carried in the Dallas papers. He was making a name for himself right here in Camden.

I gasped as a metal bridge that ran parallel to the lake came into view. "Wait. Look up there." Surrounding the bridge was heavy vegetation, but the view of the lake was splendid. The bridge framework consisted of sturdy metal beams rising gracefully above the water. Ben pulled off a few feet behind an ambulance. Confirming that not only was there a missing boat, but another victim of the hit-and-run boater.

Under the framework of the bridge, a red and white boat named "Perfect Game" grabbed my attention, with its bow wedged firmly onto the shallow section of the lake. The front of the boat pointed to the bridge as if it were running at a high speed before making a sudden stop. There was blood spatter on the boat, joining in with the red of the Runabout. A life jacket hung precariously over the edge, either loosened by the wreck or thrown off by the murderous driver.

As we walked to the center of the bridge, not daring to go down the embankment and putting ourselves in the way, another car pulled up and parked on the other side of the bridge. Oliver Fielding exited the car, slamming the door behind him. Being a mortician in a small town, sometimes he was called upon to examine bodies at accidents.

As Oliver approached the embankment, I called out. "Did they call you to take care of the body?"

Oliver didn't respond, but simply looked our way. His eyes held a mixture of shock and disbelief. His shirt tail was hanging out on one side, and his normally neat hair was uncombed. Although he opened his mouth to speak, no words came out.

"Oliver?" Something was wrong. Moving, he made his way down the embankment toward a white sheet a few yards into the brush. The policemen who had been squatting next to the poor soul under the sheet quickly covered the body and rose, putting a hand up to stop him. Oliver was there to do a job. Why was he being stopped? Then the officer lifted the sheet, and Oliver let out a heartbreaking moan, bouncing across the water and echoing through the woods.

As the sheet fell to the side, I could see the mangled body of Henry Fielding.

I put my hands to my mouth, stifling a scream. Detective Sprague ran past us, working his way down the embankment, making side steps with his feet to steady his balance. The dirt and mud from the lake caked on his well-worn dress shoes.

"Do you know who it is?" Ben asked as he put an arm around my waist, and my knees buckled.

"It's Henry. My God. I have to go down there. Oliver shouldn't be seeing this. He needs our help."

Ben, who normally would jump up and down with the opportunity to get closer to a crime scene, held back. "I don't know, Dot. Maybe we should stay up here, out of the way."

Oliver's shoulder slumped as he gazed down at Henry's broken body. He reached out and touched his only son's forehead, pushing back the muddy hair intermingled with blood that had dried on his pale skin. I began making my way down the bank, and reluctantly, Ben followed behind me. I would not leave Oliver alone in a moment like this. Henry was his world; his every thought was spent protecting him. He would never forgive himself.

"Come on, Oliver." Detective Sprague said in a gentle tone as he tried to pull him away.

Oliver's voice came out in a hoarse gasp. "But, I was just with him yesterday. He was alive."

As we drew nearer to the scene, I recognized one of the officers who had questioned us at the marina.

"Miss, you need to step back. We're conducting an investigation here."

"I know the deceased, and I work for his father. I'm trying to make sure he's OK." I attempted to push past him, but he stood squarely in my path.

"Sorry," he said.

Didn't he understand how much I wanted to help Oliver? Ben stepped forward. "My fiancée is also friends with officer Mary Oliva. Do you know if she will be coming to the scene?"

There was recognition in his eyes, and he nodded. "No, Sir. The only instructions I have are to keep people away from the scene of the accident. Now step back, please."

Oliver looked so forlorn, kneeling next to his son. Sprague was speaking to him in a hushed tone, trying to soothe him. The two men had worked cases together for over a decade, never expecting to be looking down at one of their own. Sprague stepped away, his hand wiping his eyes.

If I couldn't be there next to him, I could at least let him know I was here. "Oliver!" I shouted. "I'm here, Oliver. Can I do anything?"

Oliver looked up the embankment toward the sound of my voice. His skin was ashen, and his jaw trembled.

"My Henry. His head. Someone killed my Henry and just left him here." His eyes were wide as he met my gaze, and then he turned back to his son.

I brushed past the policeman before he could stop me and ran to Oliver. "Come on, Oliver. You need to let the police do their job."

Henry was barely aware of my presence and kept talking while staring at his son's lifeless body. "Who would do this? He never hurt anybody. Everybody liked him."

"Oliver." Sprague extended an unsteady hand. "Can we go up to the bridge? I need to ask you some questions about Henry." Sprague's piercing blue eyes were kind, and as he stood next to Oliver, his words were gentle. "Please, Oliver, there's nothing you can do for him now. Let us try to figure this out."

Oliver stepped away from Henry with a solemn acceptance of Sprague's words. I took his other hand, and we made our way up the hill, passing the officer on the perimeter. Once on the bridge road, Oliver placed his hands behind him on the uppermost rail.

Sprague spoke, his tone low and steady. "Oliver, I know this is a shock for you, but can you tell me what Henry might have been doing in the last twenty-four hours?"

Oliver let out a heavy sigh. "He went out. He told me he would be back by midnight. He usually goes out with his friend Nelson, but they had an argument, and I don't know what was going on. I just assumed they made up and went out anyway."

Sprague turned to me. "Would you know who he went out with?"

I put my hand on Oliver's shoulder. He was trembling as the shock set in. "With Nelson, I guess."

Ben came up behind me, taking out his own notebook quietly.

Sprague cleared his throat. "Excuse me. I need to question Oliver without the press recording it. You're from *The Camden Courier*, are you not?"

Ben snapped the notebook closed. "Sorry. Will you be making a statement to the press?"

"All in good time, son." He turned his focus to me. "Young lady, you need to go as well. After our past experiences in solving crimes, I know you two work as a pair." Sprague rubbed the back of his neck. He looked tired. "There are too many homicides in this little town, if you ask me. Seeing the son of a dear friend killed this way really takes it out of a guy." I backed off with Ben.

As we walked to the car, he picked up his step.

The horror of seeing Henry was creeping in on me as a tiredness seeped into my bones. "I don't think we have to run."

"I'm getting my camera. This will make a great shot for the front page."

The thought of Henry's body strewn on the bank, photographed for all of Camden to see, made me cringe.

"Ben, no. Henry was my friend. Think about what that picture will do to Oliver."

With the strap around his neck and his finger on the button, he started to speak, but no words came out at first. "Do you know what my editor will do to me if he finds out I was this close to the accident?" Ben looked at me with pleading eyes. His job was the whole reason the Dallas papers wanted him.

"I know. Why don't you take a picture of the boat running aground instead?"

Ben let out a low growl. "Fine. I'll take a picture of the boat. The way it's laid up on the bank will be something to catch the reader's eye. Sorry. I should have thought of that first." That picture would also save the dignity of little Henry Fielding, the boy who wanted so much in this life.

Chapter Six

Even though Oliver was grieving himself, he still had families to deal with at the funeral home. He sent all he could to Laughton Funeral Home in the next town and made preparations for Mrs. Garrett, who was a cremation, to have her reception through her church. Because we were slowing down operations, I was given a couple of days off. I hated to leave him alone in that big place, but he couldn't get me out the door fast enough. His mother, Neva, was so upset about Henry that she wasn't leaving her house, and Oliver mentioned something about the doctor giving her something to help her sleep. Losing one person ripples out like the waves to break many hearts.

When I called Ben to tell him of my unplanned vacation, he was ecstatic. "Great," Ben said, an eagerness in his voice. "I'm going to the hardware store to talk to Nelson White."

"You think you're going to get him to confess?"

"Maybe. I don't think the police have talked to him yet, so maybe I'll get something before they do."

"Really? They haven't talked to him? That's surprising. He's the best friend of the victim and was seen quarreling with him. Sprague must be off his game. I think Henry's death affected him deeply. He and Oliver are friends, and it must be hard to keep a professional distance when you've seen the victim grow up."

"That's true. That's why I think we need to get to Nelson. I think he's hiding something."

I remembered seeing Nelson at the fair. He was a big guy and not too happy with the new version of Henry we were seeing, but could he kill the only friend he had in the world? Every time he came into the funeral home, he acted shy around me, but he was always eager to spend time with his friend. It was the two of them against the world, or at least I had thought that was the case.

"Want to come with me?" Ben asked.

It wouldn't take much to get me to ride along on one of Ben's interviews. Being around Oliver was tearing me up. I needed a break.

We met at the hardware store before noon. The building was made of the same sturdy red brick as our courthouse, but it had a large, weathered sign hanging in front with the name Gleason's Hardware painted in bold yellow letters. In the window, they had a display of the Black and Decker FixKit for $19.98 that featured a cordless drill and sander. Its silver gleamed through the flawlessly clean window, the metal curves seducing even the most frugal home repairman. Once inside, we were greeted with the smell of wood, paint, and metal, and although the floors were clean, they creaked when we walked on them. Nelson was working behind the main counter, ringing up a bucket of paint. Behind him was a wall of tiny drawers containing screws, nails, bolts, and all those things necessary for building. Ben walked to the counter, while I took a moment to browse the store. I had been in this building many times growing up, and it always amazed me the amount of merchandise they had on the shelf. Nelson clicked the keys on the cash register as I surveyed the stacks of wood, from pine to oak, breathing in the aroma.

"Can I help you?" Nelson's voice sounded as if he were still going through the voice change of puberty. Gone was the angry young man I had seen at the fair, and in his place was a polite, competent salesman.

"I hope so," Ben said. I joined him at the counter.

Nelson looked surprised and then gave me a brief nod. "Hello, Dot."

Ben continued. "You were friends with Henry Fielding, weren't you?"

Nelson's face went from cordial to sour in seconds. "Who are you exactly?"

"Sorry," Ben said, pulling out a business card. "I'm Ben Dalton from *The Camden Courier*. Henry's father reported that the two of you had an argument on the day of his death. Can you tell me about that?"

Nelson peered at the card, looked at me, and then shot Ben a glance. "There's not much to tell. We argued, and then I left. End of story."

I had been at the funeral home working that day, typing up obituaries to deliver to the paper. I hadn't heard the argument. If Oliver hadn't told me about it, I would have never known about it. "Can I ask what you were arguing about?"

Nelson shook his head from side to side, as if the motion would shut us out. "It's not important. I wish we hadn't argued, but Henry has—" he replaced a drawer of screws in the wall behind him, "not been himself lately."

"What does that mean?" Ben said it so quickly that Nelson stepped back from the counter.

Nelson fixed on Ben's eyes as if trying to decide whether to trust him. "Are you going to put what I say in the paper? Because I don't want to do that." Nelson had every right to his privacy, and I agreed I wouldn't want the entire world to know I fought with someone right before their suspicious death. Nelson was an awkward young man and an easy target for someone to blame.

Ben leaned forward. "It would be nice to tell your side of the story in *The Camden Courier*."

"And wouldn't you just love to get that scoop?" a voice said from behind us. I turned to see a large police officer ambling toward the counter. His gut hung slightly over his belt, and two buttons looked stretched in their buttonholes. His dark hair was cut military short, and his jawline was strong even with the fullness of his face. His patch said Camden Police, but I didn't recall ever seeing him at the police station with Mary.

"How do. My name's Detective T.J. Bailey and I have a few questions for you, Mr. White."

The detective stood tall, his broad shoulders filling the room. I had never seen this man before in my life. "Pardon me," I said. "You're Camden Police? I have a friend who works there, and I don't think we've ever met."

His height was over six feet compared to my 5'4, so it was easy for him to look down on me. He pinched his round cheeks together. "I don't suppose we have. I'm new to town, replacing Sprague. It seems the murder rate around here drove him to an early retirement. Just started today."

Sometimes, life gives you a moment where things change abruptly. Here today, gone tomorrow. This was one of those moments. I liked Sprague, and I felt like he was a good detective. He was fair and open to hearing what someone had to say. This guy didn't give me that impression. More of a shoot first and ask questions later kind of guy. It was a flash judgment, so I decided the kindest thing to do would be to give him a chance. "Oh, um, nice to meet you."

"Mutual." He turned his attention back to Nelson, who was doing his best to melt into the wall.

"I hear that you and the victim had words in the afternoon before he took a ride in that boat. Want to tell me about it?"

Ben poised his pen to his notebook, ready to record every word of an actual police interview. I had seen some of his notebook pages in moments like this. He could have been a secretary taking dictations; he could get the words down on paper that fast.

Bailey's small black eyes picked up on Ben's enthusiasm for recording the interview like a hound dog for a wild rabbit. "You two can go on 'bout your business. I'm going to need some time alone with this young man."

"Sure," I said, backing out of the store.

"Any time you want to talk, Nelson," Ben said over his shoulder. "You know where I am."

Nelson didn't answer, and as I observed our newest police detective closing in, I felt sorry for him. I wondered what Mary thought of this new guy. Sprague was becoming open to having Mary along in investigations. T.J. Bailey looked like a good old boy from the word go. Good old boys rarely liked women getting in the way.

Chapter Seven

"Looks like we aren't the only ones to suspect Nelson. I have to tell my editor we have a new detective on the case." Ben kissed me on the cheek. "Will you be okay? I can drop you home."

"I'll be fine. I need to think anyway." Bluebonnets Dress Shop was only three doors away, so with time on my hands, I visited my cousin. Downtown Camden was decorated with pink flags for the upcoming Cherry Blossom Festival. They had even added pink food coloring to the town fountain, a whimsical touch by our mayor's wife. With March and spring in the air, there were plenty of brides getting on the ornery side of June wedding planning. This was the first year in a while I wasn't living through it with Ellie as my roommate, and as strange as it felt, I missed it. Couples had so many dreams when they prepared to marry, and along with that meant designing, cutting, hemming, and altering wedding dresses. I was one of those brides and should have been swept up in this Doris Day enthusiasm, but Henry's death was overshadowing thoughts of going down the aisle.

The front window of Bluebonnets displayed three bridal gowns with high necklines and long lace-covered sleeves. Next to the dresses, Ellie had placed several accessories, including veils, white gloves, and delicate headpieces encircled with pearls. The colors of the shop were pale pastels, mixed in with floral wallpaper. Women came from miles around to shop at my cousin's store and some ordered custom-made dresses for weddings.

When I entered, Ellie was standing by a young woman on top of the raised platform, looking at her figure in the mirror. The bride turned from side to side, her hands on her hips. "I don't want one of those bulky dresses. It will make me look fat, or worse, pregnant."

"Of course, we can certainly make you look thin in white," Ellie said as she artfully placated an anxious bride who didn't need to worry about her figure.

"You're sure?" The young girl had straight blond bangs falling into her eyelashes and the thinness of a fashion model.

"Sure, I'm sure. Now, you go try on this one, and then come out and let me take a look."

"If you say so," the picky bride said, folding the gown over her arm and trudging to the changing rooms.

Ellie smiled as her gaze met mine. "Finally, a bride I can't wait to work with."

It didn't surprise me she was referring to my upcoming wedding. Like my mother, every conversation we had lately ended up being about it. "Not today, but soon, I promise."

"Weren't we having this conversation in reverse last year?"

She was right. Last year, I thought Ellie was being ridiculous. We practically had to chase her down to get her to work on her dress. Maybe it was a family flaw. "I believe we were. I was just over at the hardware store and thought I'd stop by. Mr. Fielding told me to take the next couple of days off."

Ellie nodded sympathetically. "I'm sure. This is one of those times when you have to ask, why do bad things happen to good people?"

The doorbell jingled behind us, and Ellie, who had been leaning on the counter, stood up and smiled. "Mrs. Doggett! I was hoping you'd stop by. Wait till you see your dress. For you, I pulled out all the stops."

Mrs. Doggett had to be in her fifties and married, so it piqued my interest that she was buying a dress from Ellie.

"You'll be the best mother of the groom out there. Pam was just in here, picking up her wedding dress and veil. I can't believe we got it together before your oldest son left for Vietnam. It will be a beautiful, but quick, wedding."

Mrs. Doggett let out a ragged breath. "I'm afraid there's a problem."

Ellie bobbed her head forward slightly. "Oh no, did they call off the wedding?"

"No, but, well, this is so embarrassing." A tear rolled down Mrs. Doggett's cheek. I've seen women cry before, but when the most beloved lunch lady in Camden sheds a tear, it's sad to see.

Ellie came around the counter and put a hand on Mrs. Doggett's shoulder. "Come on, it can't be that bad. What happened?"

"I can't pay you. The money I saved for this dress is gone. Buck told me I didn't need a new dress for the wedding because it was too expensive, but I had my mad money I'd been saving for a rainy day, and I had planned to use that to pay you. I saved a dollar here, and a quarter there, and after a while, it added up." She stopped for a second as her voice broke. "It's gone. I'm so sorry."

"Now, now," Ellie said. "Are you sure? Maybe you just misplaced it."

She shrugged, her shoulders rounding. "No. I looked everywhere. The can is empty."

The thought of my lunch lady saving money in a can and then losing it made me instantly feel generous. There were years of brownies she had placed on my tray that made me feel like I'd step in front of a bus for her. "How much do you need?"

Mrs. Doggett looked confused. "For the dress? I can't ask you to do that."

"You don't need to ask me. I'm offering. How much?"

"Uh." She looked down while pressing her lips together.

"I know how much," Ellie said. "And what Dot doesn't cover, I will. We can't have our favorite lunch lady go down the aisle in an old dress when she has the chance to wear a Bluebonnets original."

Upon hearing our offer to cover the cost of the dress, Margaret Doggett broke into full-blown sobs, which did little for the young woman stepping out of the changing room in a wedding dress. She was already a nervous bride, so seeing someone in tears couldn't help. Her kohl-lined eyes widened under the blond fringe.

"Hold on one minute. I'll be back with your dress, Mrs. Doggett." Ellie went over to her bride and began pinching various parts of the wedding gown, promising a custom fit.

"I'm so sorry this happened to you," I whispered. "What do you think might have happened to the money?"

She dabbed at her eyes with a hanky. "I'm not sure. No one else knows about it but my family. Maybe Buck didn't want me wasting it on the dress."

"Oh, well, that's silly. Everybody needs a new dress when their son is getting married."

She nodded through bleary eyes. "I can't thank you enough."

After Mrs. Doggett left, and the skinny bride was satisfied with her order, I finally had time to give details to Ellie about finding Henry at the lake.

"I heard about it from the bakery. Everyone in the downtown stores is talking about it. Oh my God. Poor Oliver. He's spent his life taking care of that boy. What will he do now?" As she spoke, Ellie straightened several spools of ribbon from behind the counter. She was rolling up a spool of white lace with delicate pearls intricately stitched around the edging when she wobbled. She reached over and steadied herself on the edge of the counter.

"You don't look so good." As if to confirm my fears, Ellie fell to the floor in a heap.

"Ellie!" I bent to her fallen body and shook her shoulders gently. She was out. Her skin was clammy.

I ran to the phone and dialed Al. After a quick explanation of the state of his wife, he yelled into the phone. "Call an ambulance. I'll meet you at the hospital."

I hung up and dialed the ambulance. A few minutes later, a red and white station wagon that was scarily the same shape as Fielding Funeral Home's hearse pulled into the slanted park in front of the store. The red light on the top kept spinning, even though the siren wound down.

Right as they rolled in the collapsible silver stretcher into Bluebonnets, Ellie started coming to. "Uh, what happened?" She looked up at the ambulance attendant and gave a confused but friendly smile. "Hi, Ed. What are you doing here?"

Ed was probably one of her bridal party customers. Half the town was.

"I'm here to check on my wife's favorite seamstress." From there, he asked her questions before rolling her out to the ambulance.

When we arrived at Camden General Hospital, Al stood in front of the emergency entrance. Our hospital was built in the late thirties and was being outfitted for central air. Meanwhile, boxy air conditioners were scattered in the windows of the patient rooms.

"Ellie? What happened?" Al grabbed her hand as they lowered the stretcher from the back of the ambulance, extending its wheels.

"I'm not really sure," she answered.

"I saw it," I said. "She was standing there talking, and suddenly, boom, she hit the ground."

"So, she fainted?" He looked confused, and Eddie, the ambulance attendant, started pushing the stretcher into the hospital.

Ellie protested. "I don't know why they have me in this thing. I feel fine now."

We trailed after the stretcher as Ellie began unfastening the straps that held her in place. Eddie stopped her. "I wouldn't do that if I were you. You could tumble right out. Let's let the doctors decide if you're well enough to go home."

"Really. This is so silly," Ellie assured us as she continued her efforts to get off the stretcher. Suddenly, she stopped, looked down, squeezed her eyes shut, and then laid back.

"Ellie?" Al asked. "What just happened? Are you okay? Are you going to pass out again?"

Ellie paled. "Nothing, I think. Let's just talk to the doctor."

"Ellie Monroe," a gravelly female voice I immediately recognized as my aunt Mavis sang out from behind me. "You just sit still and do what they say, young lady."

"Yes, mama," she answered as they rolled Ellie down the hall to the emergency room. Eddie was hurrying, but our assembled group was matching his pace.

"That's the ticket." No one disobeyed Aunt Mavis. Especially her daughter.

"What kind of report did we get from the medic?" Mavis asked.

My aunt served in World War II, and a part of her never left the service. You could see it in everything she did. She dearly loved and cared for my uncle, but he was a loving subordinate to his commanding wife.

"That would be me, "a young doctor said, standing in the doorway. "If I could have a moment alone with my patient."

Mavis bristled. "There's nothing you could say that I haven't heard before."

"Mama," Ellie said, "give us a moment of privacy. I need to handle this without anyone else there. I'll be fine."

"Fine. Everyone, clear out."

Even though Al was Ellie's husband, he obeyed his mother-in-law's order. Before leaving, though, he doubled back and squeezed Ellie's hand.

"It'll be okay," he whispered.

Mavis went off to see if one of her gal pals from the Navy was working at the information desk. Even though her group of female friends were in their sixties, they all still tried to help the community where they could. Mavis logged hours herself, helping visitors find their loved ones at the hospital. Al and I sat in the waiting room, sipping on cups of coffee that were so strong and bitter that I coughed.

"Don't you faint on me too," Al said as he patted my back.

"I'll be fine, but I am worried about Ellie."

"Me too. This is not like her."

I absent-mindedly took another sip and then set the cup on the table. "So, I suppose you heard about the boat accident?"

Al put his cup down and pulled a Marlboro out of his pocket, along with a Zippo lighter. "Just some stuff from around town. I was waiting for the full version from Ellie. I hear about the perils of Cousin Dot almost nightly."

"Sorry about that."

"Hey, you're better than the Jack Paar show any day. How did that kid end up dead on the shore?"

"No one knows yet, but the boat was stolen."

"You don't say."

"How hard do you think it would be to steal a boat?"

"You mean, if you didn't have a key? I guess it would be like stealing a car. Anyone with basic electrical knowledge could figure out how to do it."

"Like, maybe a kid who works in a hardware store?"

"Most definitely."

I thought of Nelson White and how angry he was with Henry.

A doctor entered the waiting area and moved to Al. "Excuse me, you can go in now. Ellie wants to speak with you."

Al turned to me and said, "You may as well come along, too. She'll just tell you later, anyway."

When we entered the room, Ellie was crying. Somehow Aunt Mavis had snuck back in, and she held her daughter's hand.

"What happened?" Al said, rushing to the other side of the bed.

"We're pregnant." Ellie looked amazed, as if somewhere Aunt Mavis had forgotten to give her the talk about the birds and the bees.

"We are? Really? Oh, Ellie. You mean, that's why you've been so tired? We're going to have a baby." Al pulled her into a hug, nearly lifting her out of the bed. "Oh gosh. Sorry. Are you okay now?" He gently lowered her back to the bed.

"Better than okay," Aunt Mavis said.

"I didn't even know I was pregnant. I was a little tired, but we are at the beginning of wedding season, so I thought nothing of it."

"That's the problem, El," Al said. "You are getting those engines fired up for the new brides every year, and don't think about the toll it takes on you." He grabbed her hand. "From now on, we think of the baby first."

Seeing her fall to the floor this morning scared me. I was still in shock at the thought of my cousin needing an ambulance. I pushed past Al and gave Ellie a hug. "A baby. It couldn't happen to two nicer people."

"Thank goodness you were there with her. It might have been quite a while before a customer discovered her," Al said.

"Yes, especially considering our Dot gets to people too late. I heard you found another body. You're getting quite a reputation." Aunt Mavis said.

"Technically, it wasn't just me, but me and Ben. Henry Fielding."

"And," Mavis continued, "this is another work-related death for you. I don't want to be overly negative, but I think people in this town will think twice about hiring you next time."

Ellie snorted. "Don't be silly, mother. It's not that bad."

"Yes, it is," Al said, smiling, "but let's not talk about that. I'm going to be a daddy."

I tried to disregard what my aunt just said about my reputation. She was exaggerating, but still, I suddenly had a desire to visit the hardware store and have another discussion with Nelson White. He had the means and the motive to kill Henry, and if he were the only true friend Henry had in this world, I would personally make sure that the police knew. I couldn't do this alone. I would call Ben to see if he would tag along with me. I still couldn't believe he had the guts to do anything like that, which made me question: who else might have done it? Who had anger so deep they could kill? Who had Henry come up against the weeks before his death?

Chapter Eight

Using the pay phone in the hospital's lobby, I called Ben. When he answered, he sounded distracted, and typewriters clacked in the background. In the layout of the work area of the newspaper office, instead of having a private office, the desks were in one expansive room, which made it hard to hear if more than one reporter was typing to meet a deadline. "What do you mean you want to go back and talk to this Nelson boy again?" he asked, raising his voice over the din. "Haven't we already done that? My editor said I didn't have anything on Nelson, and writing a story on him would border on harassment."

"Yes, we did, but when I was talking to Al at the hospital, he told me that anybody who worked in a hardware store could also figure out how to steal a boat pretty easily."

Ben cut off my sentence. "Back up. Why were you at the hospital with Al?"

"I can't go into too much detail, but Ellie fainted."

"Is she pregnant?" I knew Ben was an excellent reporter, but how could he know already?

"Why would you say that?"

"Because every single series I've watched on television in the last ten years has shown a newly married woman faint, and it always ends up she's pregnant."

I didn't think he had even been watching those shows, but Ben was good at picking up on clues. "God. You're right. She's pregnant, but I was trying to let her tell people."

"I'm not people; I'm practically family," he said. "How is Al taking it?"

50

"He's happy, but we had to wait in the lobby while the doctor examined Ellie. That was how I ended up talking to Al about how much knowledge it takes to steal a boat. That led me back to Nelson. Think about it. He and Henry had an argument, and he's angry, and he can steal a boat. I want to ask him some more questions, but I don't feel comfortable asking him alone."

"Smart girl. I need to finish something up here. Why don't I meet you in about half an hour?"

"Okay. I'll get a ride home to get my car and then meet you there."

Once Aunt Mavis dropped me off at my apartment, I hopped in my car and headed back downtown. I parked in the slanted parking lot in front of the hardware store. I could see Nelson in the windows, and because it was stuffy in my car, I unrolled the window down to get a breeze passing through while I waited. Soon, I heard male voices hooting and hollering in the distance. I turned around, and Jeff and Chad stood across the street behind me as they leaned on the wall next to the Army recruiter's office. It was in a small space that used to be a bookstore in town, but it had never found another stable tenant until the US Army took it over. The recruitment center had been there for about a year since the Vietnam conflict started heating up. Chad said something I couldn't hear, then Jeff laughed like he was sitting in the front row at a Lenny Bruce show listening to the latest one-liners. That was the thing with these two; there was always an inside joke between them, often at the sacrifice of others. Whenever other girls acted like that around me at school, I tried to avoid them. You had only to get on their radar, and they would hurt your feelings. Other people's feelings are cheap currency for some people. Easily expendable and soon forgotten.

From a distance, I could tell they were making fun of the Army recruiter's office. At the funeral, Chad's mother had said that his father expected him to go into the service the way his brother had. From the looks of it, Chad wasn't taking voluntary service seriously.

"Whatcha doing?" Ben stood in front of my car. I rolled up my window and got out, joining him on the sidewalk.

"I'm waiting for you and watching those two," I said in a hushed voice.

Ben looked over. "Chuckle heads. Well, I'm here now, so let's go get this over with."

When we entered the hardware store, Nelson was busy stacking white paint into a perfect pyramid. He turned around and smiled at our footsteps; then his lips flattened into a frown.

"Hello, Dot. I'm surprised to see you again." His voice sloped upward when he said my name. He swallowed, looking uncomfortable.

"I wanted to ask you a couple more questions," I said.

"I don't know what you would want to ask me. Henry was my friend, and now he's gone. I really don't want to discuss this anymore."

Ben took a step forward. "I think you're skipping a few of the details here. Anything new you want to tell us that you shared with our town's newest detective? Did he get a confession out of you? He looked like the type who wouldn't mind pushing a suspect."

Nelson's face grew red. "I held my own. Just what are you implying? You think I would kill my friend just because we had an argument? If you think that, you obviously don't understand the concept of having a best friend."

Nelson was getting angry, probably because it was our second visit in one day. If he blew up, we wouldn't get anywhere. I tried to use a more conversational tone with him. "Do you sell parts for people who are working on boats here?"

Nelson bit his bottom lip and put his hands in his pockets. "I suppose so. Why does it matter?"

"Have you ever worked on a boat?" Ben came back at him with rapid fire.

"Sure. I've worked on a few," Nelson admitted.

So, Nelson knew enough about boats to fix them, and he could probably start one without a key. Still, as I looked at this pimply-faced young man, I couldn't imagine him as a killer.

"If that's all you want to know, I have things to do here." He turned back to the paint cans.

We were being dismissed with little information. If Nelson wasn't the murderer, maybe he knew who was. I stopped abruptly, making Ben bump into me. "Do you know anybody else who would want to kill Henry?"

Nelson still didn't turn around but looked down at his hands. "Henry was a good guy. Too good for some of the likes of people around here."

"What does that mean?"

"You figure it out." He went back to his chore, using it to ignore us. Another customer entered the store, and Nelson switched on the charm. "Hello, Mrs. Martin. Need more paint for the nursery you're fixing up?"

After leaving the hardware store, we went out onto the street. Nelson's last words had me puzzled, and I wanted to know what he was holding back from us.

"What do you think that was all about?" Ben asked.

"I'm not really sure, but there is a lot more going on than what that guy is telling us. He was Henry's best and only friend, but some of his comments didn't sound like someone who's still grieving. He sounds like someone who's angry. I'm not sure why they were fighting, but he was wounded somehow."

"Wounded enough to want to kill Henry? He's just a kid."

"That was the whole reason I brought you here today. He had the means to kill him. He knew all about boats and engines, so why not make it an accident and try to pawn it off as the same person who killed Betty Weaver?"

Ben put a finger to his chin in thought. "I don't know. It seems pretty evil for a guy like that."

"I agree, but you never know what makes a person murder. Sometimes, people murder other people for things you or I would think of as trivial. A slight, a blunder, the feeling of being left out. Not a big deal to most people, but to a potential killer, it's unforgivable."

As we stood outside the hardware store, the wind picked up around us, and the hearse from Fielding Funeral Home rolled by us down the street. Behind the wheel, Oliver looked straight ahead.

"There's Oliver. He was shutting down the funeral home for a couple of days, so I wonder what he was doing with the hearse?"

Ben put his hands in his pockets. "Maybe he went to put gas in it?"

"But Henry just gassed up the hearse the other day. Remember? It took him two hours to do it."

"Two hours? How much gas does a hearse take?"

"Exactly. Henry never explained where he went during that time, but I'll bet it has to do with all these questions we can't get answered."

"Okay, you're saying driving the hearse can lead to bad things?"

"I just hope that doesn't extend to Oliver. I'm so worried about him. His mother, Neva, is there, but she's not his son. Henry was what Oliver lived for. I don't know what he'll do now. Oliver is gifted at helping other people through painful mourning, but I'm not sure who will be there to help him through his."

"You'll be there for him."

"I guess, but I've only worked at the funeral home for a short time."

"What I want to know is what was Henry Fielding really doing in those two hours he went AWOL?"

"Whatever he was doing, he was doing it with a great big black hearse, which means wherever he was, someone must have seen the car."

"And whoever saw the car has no idea they're sitting on top of what might solve a murder."

All these questions were spinning around in my head. I needed to take a little time to think it through. I kissed Ben on the cheek. He turned and pulled me into his arms. It was such a nice place to be. "Thanks for coming with me today. You go work on your story, and I'm going home to put my feet up. Tomorrow morning, I think I'll stop by the funeral home to check on Oliver. I'm worried about him. He really has nobody in this world now that Henry is gone."

"Good idea, and while you're there, see if you can find out where Henry went with the hearse that day."

Chapter Nine

The next morning, even though I didn't have to be at work, I used my key and unlocked the back door at Fielding Funeral Home. As I walked through the rooms lit with only a few beams of light from the velvet drapes, a shiver ran down my spine, as if the very essence of grief floated through the air. I worried that something was getting ready to jump out at me. The faint aroma of funeral flowers lingered around me. I had never worried about the ghosts of past clients haunting the funeral home, but today, it seemed plausible. I felt the collective sorrow of countless mourners who had passed through its doors. Like an empty theater, this was not a good place to be alone. I heard a sound in the walls and looked over my shoulder. I had to stop this. Probably settling wood or something banging in the pipes. It was funny how the funeral home felt different when I was the only one there. I flicked the light switch on the wall. "Oliver? Are you here?"

It was a stupid question to ask because Oliver's car was not in the parking lot. He drove a blue Chevy station wagon when he was not driving the hearse.

Without Henry to help Oliver, things might have started to get disorganized, so I made sure there was nothing pending on Henry's desk. Almost everything he did was under the direction of his father, but something like ordering supplies might slip by Oliver in his grief.

Henry's desk was downstairs, right next to the embalming room. Even though the ventilation system was state-of-the-art, the disinfectant smell of chemicals hung in the air. The location of this office was important, as Henry oversaw deliveries of both the deceased and the supplies. I made my way down the stairs, turning on the light switch first this time.

Henry had been neat, but there were a couple of invoices on his desk. I picked them up, intending to put them in a file folder for Oliver to attend to. Under the invoices, I found an application for enlistment in the US Army. The application was blank, but it raised a question. Had Henry been planning to join the Army? Was that what he had been so happy about at Betty Weaver's funeral reception? I wondered if Oliver knew anything about Henry's plans. He was so protective of Henry, I had a hard time believing he would support anything like joining the Army.

Oliver had been on top of his son's life. He told me about making sure he was at all of Henry's school activities, even if there was a funeral on the books. He was proud of his son but also very aware of people who might not be welcoming to the kid who wore a hearing aid. People often assume that just because Henry couldn't hear, he also had a low IQ. Henry hated this treatment the most, especially when they started speaking to him like he was a small child.

I heard footsteps upstairs. This time, it sounded like an actual living person. "Oliver? Is that you? I'm downstairs."

The sound of heavy footsteps echoed through the house as they made their way steadily down into the basement. Oliver stood in the doorway of Henry's office. Normally, he could have been a model for the J. C. Penney men's business wear section. He wore crisp dark suits with white starched button-down shirts, always accompanied by a discreet necktie. When he and Henry were about to open the doors to a visitation, I'd seen him pull a portable lint roller out of a drawer to remove any stray particles from his son's suit. Today, all of that was gone. He wore a white shirt, but it was wrinkled as if he had slept in it. No tie. No jacket. From the circles under his eyes, he probably had. "Dot? What are you doing here?" His voice was gruff.

"I know you told me to take some time off, but I thought I'd make sure there wasn't anything important on Henry's desk."

He let out a tired sigh. There was so much sadness in his eyes. "That's very thoughtful of you, dear. Is there anything I need to know about?"

"A couple of invoices and, um," I produced the application for the Army. "There was this." I handed it to him. "Did you know Henry was thinking about joining the Army?"

Oliver read down the page, his brow wrinkling. "The Army? This must be a mistake. Henry never said anything about joining the Army. Come on, Dot. He's not the type who joins the Army. He didn't even like camping when he was a Boy Scout."

"Then why did he have this application?"

"I don't know."

"I'm not sure if you noticed, but there was something different about Henry the week before he died."

Oliver looked up from the application. "What was that? I didn't notice anything. I only wish I had. If I'd paid more attention to what he was doing, he might be alive today."

What I had seen were subtle behavior changes. Nothing I could put my finger on. I felt foolish for even bringing it up, mostly because I could be making something out of nothing." I don't know. His mood? Henry never seemed happy about anything in his life. At Betty Weaver's funeral, he was practically giddy. After finding this application, do you think he was thinking about joining the Army and fighting in Vietnam? I can't believe that would make him happy, but young men get excited about going to war."

Oliver shook his head in confusion. "No. Henry would never have done anything this dangerous. I raised him. He was not a risk taker."

"What would have been too dangerous?" Neva Field stood in the doorway to Henry's former office. She was dressed in her normal funeral home attire of a sedate black dress and white pearls. Unlike her son, she had returned to her standard dress code. In her hand, she carried the metal watering can. Had she been the noises I had heard earlier?

"Mother? I didn't know you were here," Oliver said.

"Well, someone has to keep the plants alive." She emphasized the word "someone" as she looked my way. "Now, what was dangerous? Have you uncovered something that could tell us who killed Henry?"

Oliver held up the Army application. "This was on his desk. Did he ever say anything to you about enlisting?"

Neva set down the can and snatched the application out of Oliver's hand.

"Of course not. What a ridiculous idea. That boy already had a career path carrying on the running of the funeral home. I don't know why this was on his desk, but no grandson of mine goes to war to kill people. He was raised to respect the dead. He would never take another person's life."

"Maybe I drove him to it," Oliver said. "As a father, you never want your son to have a moment of unhappiness, and you also never want him to leave home. Was it so bad here that he was willing to fight in a war halfway across the world?"

"I find that hard to believe. You were always a wonderful father to Henry."

"Was I? Really? When Henry came back from filling up the hearse there was almost a fourth of a tank gone already. I took the hearse out and tried to figure out how far that would be. Now that we see this application, maybe it was Dallas. Maybe that's where he went to get it. No one would think twice about a hearse from out of town pulling up to the recruiting office."

Oliver's theory explained the amount of time Henry was missing. I straightened the green blotter on Henry's desk. Once moved, there was a small stack of wrinkled dollars sticking out from underneath the leather edge. "What's this?" I pulled out the assortment of bills. Why had Henry hidden so much money under his desk pad?

"Where would Henry get that kind of money?" Neva asked.

"Maybe it's from a paycheck." I offered.

"Hardly. He doesn't make that much."

"Then where did he get this?" I asked.

"I don't know, but something tells me it might have had to do with his death." Oliver's voice cracked. "I tried so hard to guide him and protect him. If my ex-wife had been here, she might have done a better job of raising him. What kind of father raises a child around a funeral home? Did Oliver ever tell you about his mother?"

Neva snorted. "And now we're going to talk about her. She never belonged here. She wasn't one of us, and I made sure she knew it." Neva picked up the watering can. "As long as you're here, Dot, the rooms could use dusting." With that, she climbed the stairs back to the main floor.

I had wondered why they were two bachelors living together, but hadn't dared to ask. Oliver continued.

"My ex-wife, Florence, doesn't live in Texas. She's in New York now. We were high school sweethearts and found ourselves pregnant in our senior year. We married, and I finished school. When Henry was born and diagnosed with hearing loss, she had trouble with it. Then, on top of that, her Prince Charming was following in the family business. Not very romantic living with a mortician. After a year of being unhappy, she left. She finished her high school degree and then went to college. At first, we shared custody of Henry, but his primary residence was with me. Florence was busy with school, and then she remarried. She has two more children now. She sees, or I guess I should say saw Henry, once a year in the summer. I know Henry wanted more, but that was all she was willing to give. My mother has tried to fill the void, but it wasn't the same, you know? I wish I could have been a better father. Maybe then he wouldn't be dead now."

My gaze met Oliver's. "Whatever happened with Henry is not your fault."

Oliver walked over and sat in Henry's chair, running his hands along the wooden armrests. "Maybe I was too protective. Maybe that's why he was unhappy."

"Please don't say that. You did what you thought was right." I handed the money to Oliver. "We'll figure this out, and when we do, we will catch whoever did this to Henry."

Oliver gave a weak smile. "Thanks. and thanks for checking Henry's desk. My head is not on business. The funeral will be on Friday over at Laughton Funeral Home. We'll stay closed until Monday. You can take a few more days off, with pay, of course."

"No, you can't afford that. I'll be fine."

"Something a funeral home director should never say, but business has been good. We can pay you. Other things around here will never be the same without Henry. Thanks again. Henry should have gotten to know you better, Dot."

Henry and I had worked closely together, but I couldn't say we were friends. Even though we were only about five years apart in age, he still had the maturity level of a high school boy. He felt like a little brother. I needed to go back to the details of his death. If I couldn't get information from Nelson White, I might look at the crime scene.

Chapter Ten

After leaving Oliver, I decided to speak to the marina owner one more time to try to figure out who took the boat used in Henry's murder. Grabbing a sandwich at my apartment, I called Ben to see if he would like to go along with me. He was covering court this week for a reporter on vacation, so I was lucky to catch him at his desk.

"Yes, I'd love to go with you, and as luck would have it, the judge rescheduled the court case."

Even though some people might think a reporter's life is glamorous and full of intrigue, Ben was covering a case of stolen pigs for *The Camden Courier*. Shorty Wyckoff, a pig farmer, claimed Bill Wheeler, another pig farmer, snuck up in the cloak of darkness and loaded up an 1100-pound sow into the back of a pickup truck. What made her so valuable was her nickname, Fertile Myrtle. It was reported that she could get pregnant with only one try, and the results were dozens of little piggies. The newspaper had dubbed the case "Makin' Bacon Caper." It was a popular series of articles, considering it was one step up from the farm report and featured the sex lives of pigs.

"I'll pick you up, but I have to warn you, ol' Bernice isn't doing too well. I think she's on her last breath."

"Ol' Bernice, a 1955 Oldsmobile, had several dents, bald tires, and a constant wheezing coming out from under the rusty brown hood. "Should we take my car?"

"Nice of you to offer, but I want to take Bernice today. I have plans for her."

Besides setting her on fire or pushing her off the nearest cliff, I wasn't sure what he had in mind. I knew Ben had arrived when I heard the familiar wheezing and sputtering of Bernice in my driveway.

Ben and I returned to the marina, but this time, the marina owner was nowhere to be found. The marina office and residence stood atop a small hill overlooking the glistening waters of the bay. Selma, the guard dog Shep had praised, did not bark or even growl, but playfully nudged her snout against my hand, her tail wagging vigorously in excitement. We knocked on the glass panes of the marina office, and after not getting an answer, I clasped my hands around my eyes and, leaning on the glass, looked inside. As I drew closer, I could hear the low rumble of jazz, heavy on the bass. It created a melodic backdrop with the gentle lapping of the waves. "I think he must be farther back in the house. I hear a stereo."

Ben put his ear to the glass and then turned around to face the parking lot. "Hmmm. How many cars do you see parked here?"

I turned back and scanned the parking area. "Three."

"Right. Ours, his, and whose is that?" He pointed at a wood-paneled station wagon. It was the kind of car a family with children would use.

"I don't know. I didn't see anyone else around here. Maybe someone has taken their boat out."

"Maybe, but when we were here last, there were twelve boats in twelve boat slips. Today, I only see eleven. Considering Bubba Jenkins's boat—was just impounded for a murder investigation. I would say all the remaining boats are here."

"Which means whoever is driving that station wagon is inside, listening to jazz with Shep. Let's try knocking at the backdoor," I said.

We made our way around, and as we did, the sound of the music grew louder, along with a few other sounds.

Ben smiled and blushed a little as we heard rhythmic moans coming from an open window. "They must be big music lovers."

I giggled. "Regular jazz nuts." There was no doubt about what they were doing, and from the sounds of it, things were going quite well.

Ben raised his hand to knock, but then stopped. "Not the best time."

"Yeah. Maybe we can figure this out on our own. I don't think I could erase a memory of hot and sweaty Shep, but I am curious about who he has in there with him."

"Let's go look at the boats." We walked around the house to the parking lot. Selma followed along, her tail still wagging. As the jazz and the sound of other things faded in my ears, I asked Ben, "What exactly are we looking for?"

"I'm not sure, just something out of the ordinary. Maybe Henry's killer left something important on the dock."

"You mean like his I.D.? That would make things easier. Do you know a lot about boats? We didn't do much boating at our house, although I have been waterskiing with friends."

"A little." He shrugged. "Not much. We need to concentrate, and hearing about you in a bathing suit is not making my thoughts flow."

I giggled. "Billie Holiday will do that to a person."

We walked on the wooden pier as the surrounding water was still. There was little call to take a boat out on a weekday. The boats were in a variety of sizes, but most were small speedboats with a pontoon moored at the end. Inside a few boats, there were remnants of beer bottles and sandwich wrappers.

"Not very tidy, these boat people, and from the looks of the empty beer bottles, there are several drunk drivers out on the lake at the same time. No wonder Betty Weaver got hit," I said, walking to the end of the pier. The pontoon was covered with a canvas drape. Looking underneath, the insides were as neat as a pin.

"Look at this," Ben said, crouched down by the tip of a small speedboat. "It looks like they've sustained some damage here."

On the side of the boat, a scrape had cut through the sleek paint, making a line through the boat name, *Lucky Me*. Not as lucky as the boat owner might have thought.

"So, somebody isn't very good at putting the boat back into the dock. I hardly think that has anything to do with boat thefts."

Ben nodded. "You're probably right, but we know there has been a boat thief out here. What's to say this person only used one boat?"

"You mean like a serial boat thief?" Could a person get away with stealing different boats periodically from the marina? Was starting one boat as easy as starting another?

"Think about it," Ben said. "Just how many days a week are Romeo and Juliet in there playing Billie Holiday on the stereo?"

The boat dock was at least fifty yards from the combined house and office. Someone could be out here starting a boat, and if the marina owner was busy, he would hear nothing. "He wouldn't hear it, and Selma, the guard dog, gets put outside on occasions, so happy for a visitor, she doesn't even bark."

Ben snapped his fingers. "Bubba Jenkins is Al's friend, right? We need to talk to him. He might be sitting on information."

"You know, Al has mentioned him, but I'm not sure what he does."

"Then we'll have to ask him."

As we turned to head back to Ben's car, the sound of a screen door opening peeled through the air. Shep, his cheeks rosy and his shirt half on, edged around from the back of the house and immediately spotted Ben's car. His gaze shifted to the dock.

"Can I help you, folks? How long have you been standing out here?"

I walked forward. "We tried knocking, but there was no answer."

"Yes, you must have been busy," Ben said.

Shep lifted his chin slightly. "Working on the books. Guess I got involved. Numbers are not my thing."

We knew just what his thing was.

Ben walked forward and extended his hand. "Ben Dalton, *Camden Courier*."

Shep reached out with a measured amount of enthusiasm. "I remember you. What can I do for you this time?"

"We were wondering if you could provide a list of the boat owners here at the marina. I would also like to get in touch with Bubba Jenkins. Ben said this with such efficiency. Shep let go of his hand and stepped back.

"Why would I do that?"

Ben swept his hand back toward the boats. "In the interest of the investigation. Two deaths on the water don't exactly put the security of your marina in a good light."

Shep raised a single finger in the air and shook it at Ben's face. "Lookie here, son. If I hand over a list like that, it will be to the police, and only the police will get it. Hear me? You and your lady friend need to quit nosin' around here. If I see you again, I'll call the cops on you for trespassing. Get me?"

"This is public property. There's not much you can do."

"Watch me."

"You seemed more than willing to let people nose around and steal other people's boats. I think you're a little late with your righteous indignation," I said.

"Yeah, well, a tiger can change its spots. I don't need a lot of folks here getting into my business." He glanced up at the house. "Talking to you has been a mistake, and now I'm fixing it. Out with you."

As we made our way to the car, Ben turned and spoke. "We're leaving, but remember, if you ever want to talk—"

"Out!"

The drive into town was quiet except for the sounds of Bernice's wheezing and clanking as it lumbered down the road. Ben tapped the steering wheel with a finger, deep in thought.

"So, do we find Al to ask about his friend Bubba? He could be anywhere in town doing electrical work. I suppose we could ask Ellie."

"Yes, but I need to make a stop first."

We drove through downtown Camden, and at the end of Main Street, Ben pulled into Big Buck's Ford Sales and Service. Blue flags were strung in an x across the parking lot, with the Ford logo encased in matching blue and shining above the Big Buck's sign. Everyone in town either bought their car here or over at Camden Chevy, depending on which school of thought a driver might belong to. The tailfins of the '50s weren't completely gone, but they made a more subtle line on the powerful v8 engines of the Galaxies, Fairlanes, and the top-of-the-line Thunderbirds. Ben parked and jumped out of the car. He made a beeline for a row of Mustangs, finally stopping in front of a silver-blue one.

"Isn't this the most beautiful car you've ever seen?"

It was beautiful, and even more, it was sleek, low to the ground, and felt like now.

Ben continued, not waiting for my answer. "Just look at this, baby. V-8 engine, GT, four-speed." He caressed the side of the car along the door panel. "It's a convertible, too, so we could take rides in the country."

"Four seats, so we can take Al and Ellie along with us. It's perfect."

I visualized myself, like Princess Grace with her sheer scarf, looking glamorous in the front seat of this man-made wonder.

"She's a beaut, isn't she?" We turned around to see Big Buck himself, a cigar sticking out of his mouth, and a sideways smile that showed his rounded reddened cheeks. He extended a hand to Ben. "Buck Doggett. How 'bout taking this baby out for a spin? She's been waiting for you all day." The gleam in his eye told me, in his mind, he'd already made a sale.

Ben stalled. "I don't know. If I drive it, I might buy it, and I already know what the price is. I've been reading your ads in the paper."

"Now, don't you worry about that. We have financing and from the looks of it," he turned back and looked at ol' Bernice, parked there in all her dilapidated glory. "You have a trade-in. We can work out a nice deal when the time comes. But for now," he pulled a set of keys out of his pockets. "Take her out. Let her show you what she's got."

Ben looked at me, the wonder of Christmas morning in his eyes, he scooped the key out of Big Buck's hands. "We'll just drive it around the block."

"Around the block? Take her out on the highway. This particular model has a terrific pickup. Besides, I'm sure your young lady would like to know what it feels like to have the breeze blow through her bee-you-ti-ful blond hair."

Ben nodded like a chicken pecking at the ground and rushed to unlock the car and open the door for me. Big Buck reached over and pushed a button to slide back the top. "Aint' she a beauty?"

Ben jumped in the driver's seat and we were off. After a few rounds of the town, Ben got out on the highway. My hair blew in the breeze, as Big Buck promised. It also blew in my eyes, causing me to have a constant hand up to brush it away. Princess Grace made this look so easy.

When we finally pulled back into the car lot, my hair resembled the Bride of Frankenstein from the old Lon Chaney movie. I tried to push it back in place, but it wasn't going there without water, hairspray, and an act of God.

Big Buck stood there, his hands in his pockets, while rocking on his feet. "Well, how did it do?"

"What a car."

Big Buck's face curved into a smile that had "sale" written all over it. "I thought you'd say something like that. What do you say? We'll step into my office and start hashing out the financing. I think you'll be pleasantly surprised at how generous our deals are."

Ben's eyes met mine. "Do you mind?"

I wasn't all that sure how long it took to trade in one car and buy another. "I guess not."

My gaze shifted to ol' Bernice. I hated to see her go. Ben picked me up with her the first time we went out on a date. We'd also steamed up the windows a couple of times. I would miss that beat-up old jalopy. As they started into the office, which was comprised of a small building with white siding and an attached garage, I noticed Chad Doggett approaching Bernice with a clipboard. He looked different without Jeff joking by his side. One stark change was that he was frowning. "Uh, Ben. I'll be in there with you in a minute, okay?" I nodded to Chad and hoped he could understand I wanted to ask him some questions. I wasn't even sure why, but he seemed wrapped up in all this stuff with being at Betty Weaver's funeral.

"Don't you worry about it, little lady," Big Buck said. "I'll have your man in that beautiful new car in no time."

I smiled, thinking Big Buck was in full-tilt sales mode. I walked over to Chad, who had been watching us as he walked around ol' Bernice, noting all her features.

"So, you work here? I didn't know that."

He looked up from the clipboard. "Not by choice. Big Buck is my dad."

"Oh, yes. I think you mentioned that at the funeral. Too bad they haven't figured out who killed Betty Weaver yet, and now there's Henry."

Chad smirked. "The Camden cops? Might as well call them the Keystone

Cops. This is way above what they've read in their junior detective manuals."

"I guess so. I was wondering. Do you know anyone who might have a boat moored out at the Camden Marina?"

He gave me a strange look, and I noticed for the first time that his eyes were a deep brown. "My dad had a boat out there for a while but doesn't anymore. He made me clean out the garage, so he keeps it there now."

This was interesting. "Did you meet anyone else out there with a boat?"

"No. Why are you asking? Thinking about putting a boat out there?" He smiled. "I never figured you for a nautical girl."

"Funny. We are trying to figure out what's happening with all of these deaths due to boat accidents. My boyfriend, uh, fiancée, is a reporter for The Camden Chronicle, and he's trying to track down leads on the case."

Chad's eyes widened. "Really? Your boyfriend is a reporter? I didn't know that."

"There' are a lot of things about me you don't know."

A mischievous look came into his eyes. "I know one thing you probably don't know, but it's pretty hilarious if you ask me. The town is calling you the Camden Curse because you seem to get people killed all the time. Your boyfriend is comfortable with that?"

It was amazing how quickly he struck a nerve. This overgrown teenager had pinpointed the one thing quietly burning a hole in me. Yes, I knew what they said about me, and yes, I worried it could affect what I had with Ben. I suddenly didn't want to talk anymore. "Well, if you hear anything about the boats, just let me know."

"Like I said. I don't know anything because it was my dad who had a boat out there, not me." Chad turned his back and went back to writing on the clipboard. I had a feeling ol' Bernice would not get a good report. Ben would be lucky if he got twenty dollars for her.

Chapter Eleven

On my third day away from the funeral home, I was feeling bored and decided I would stop in and check on Ellie at the dress shop. "Sure, I can sew. I made this dress." Barbara Olson touched her hem to point out her handiwork, holding it out for Ellie's examination. Ellie ran a hand along the applicant's shoulder seams, straightened the collar, and then turned up the hem to examine the stitches.

Ellie pinched the zipper in the back. She could spot bad stitching in an instant. "You do good work. How did you find out about this job?" Barbara, a petite woman standing at 5'1, had a pixie-style haircut that accentuated her features. When she spoke, her high, nasally voice filled the room.

I had mentioned Ellie would be hiring to my mother, who then told Ellie's mother, and from there, that piece of news was more reliable than the Associated Press ticker tapes. I was only glad to see Ellie was following through on her promise to hire someone. It had taken a pregnancy to bend her stubbornness, and maybe this child would help temper Ellie's bossiness.

The young woman's eyes brightened. "Are you kidding me? When word got out that you needed help, I jumped at the chance. Like I said, this is my favorite store. I bought all my prom dresses here, and you even shortened them for me. When you're as small as I am, it's hard to find a dress that will fit. That was when I decided that with my size, sewing was my best option."

Ellie turned to me and beamed. As the sun shone through the dress store window, I could tell Ellie's predicament had solved itself. After her unscheduled trip to the hospital, I was glad that now she could concentrate on having a baby.

"What's your name?"

"Barbara. Not Barbie, not Barb. Barbara, like Barbra Streisand, but I don't spell it that way," she said, and with her short hair, she looked like Barbra Streisand, sort of. The Texas version.

"Well, Barbara, consider yourself hired."

"Really? When can I start?"

"First thing tomorrow, if that's not too soon. We open at 9, but I want you here at 8. I need to show you how I do things with the alterations in the back room. Sound good?"

Barbara smiled. "It's a dream come true," she said, her Texas accent clipping the last word upward.

After Barbara left, I patted Ellie on the back. "You did it. Good job."

Ellie returned to her folding chair. "It was easier than I thought." As she spoke, two women who looked like mother and daughter came in, arguing about a wedding dress. Ellie's eyes rolled. End of her break.

"Do you want me to stay? I have the day off."

"No. I'll be okay. These two have been here every day this week. I'm up for whatever they throw at me." For some women, shopping was a necessity. For others, it was a maddening need to get "it" whatever "it" was, perfect.

With a few hours left on my day off, I didn't feel like going home just yet, so I decided I would drop in on Mary at the police station. I might catch her on a break. When I stepped into the Camden Police Station, I found Officer Jerry at the front desk, directing somebody on how to bail out a prisoner. I took a seat on the bench to wait. I noticed Mary was not in her usual place, filing behind the front counter. Could she have stepped out for a moment? I waited but knew when she saw me, she'd push past Jerry. A minute passed, and then two. Where was she? I stood up and looked at her desk. Normally, it was full of neatly stacked file folders. Today, the manila folders looked like they had been tossed there casually, one so close to the edge of the desk it might hit the floor. It was easy to see that Mary was no longer assigned to that desk. My first impression of T.J. Bailey had not been a good one, but that Mary was working somewhere new in the station gave me hope. Maybe the new guy recognized her for her deductive talents.

As much as I had grown to like Detective Sprague, T.J. Bailey might not be all that bad.

When the woman at the counter left to call on the town's bail bondsman, Mickey Blake, owner of Blakes Bust 'Em Out Bail Bonds, I approached Jerry.

"That poor woman…" I said. "It must be awful to have to bail out someone you love."

Officer Jerry scowled. "Well, next time, you can bet she'll think twice before getting hitched to a loser, now, won't she?"

Officer Jerry's outlook on the world was heavily influenced by the wise-cracking Joe Friday on Dragnet. Except he had no compassion. No understanding, just a lousy opinion I didn't particularly want to hear. Before he could further tell me about other poor souls who had crossed his path today, I got to the point of my visit. "Where's Mary?"

A little smile curled the side of Officer Jerry's mouth. "Didn't you hear? They got her doing dispatch."

"Dispatch? I didn't know police officers worked that job."

His grin grew bigger. "They don't." He wiggled his eyebrows, clearly pleased to let me know Mary was doing a job she hadn't trained at the academy for. "She's two doors down the hall with the other gal." He made a dismissive motion with his hand. He couldn't stop grinning. Mary had gone from his area, and he was happy about it.

I looked over at the messy desk full of teetering files. "It's too bad they're asking you to work at the front desk and handle that big stack of filing. Mary made it look so easy, but of course, we gals are so much better at organization than you fellas."

Officer Jerry sneered at me. "Oh, don't you worry, I'll ask her real nice to clean up that mess. After all, I am now her superior, aren't I?"

I passed him, resisting the urge to punch an officer of the law. I glanced into the offices I passed and finally found Mary twirling the plastic phone cord as she spoke into the phone. There was another lady beside her, eating a cookie.

"Car 4, we have a welfare check at Mrs. Baum's house again."

A static-filled voice answered back over the radio. "Roger that, Mary. We'll head over."

Mary closed out the call, looked up, and then smiled. "You're a welcome sight for sore eyes." She turned to her coworker, who was knocking cookie crumbs off her blouse. "I'm going on a break. Back in ten."

She led me to a small lunchroom at the back of the station. There was a Coke machine, a refrigerator, a white linoleum counter, and two matching tables. A coffee pot sat on the counter, and a set of mugs were drying on a dish rack next to the sink. "What brings you down here? Want to report a crime?" Mary put a dime in the Coke machine. "Can I get you one? I have another dime."

I waved her off. "No, I'm fine. How long have you been working in dispatch?"

Mary popped the top of her soda, took a drink, and shrugged. She put her pull tab in a large gray metal can. "Since last week, it seems our new detective Bailey had a problem with my role in investigations with Detective Sprague and told the chief women only excel when they talk on the phone. So here I am."

"But, Mary, this isn't what you trained for."

"Tell me about it. We're just lucky our police station doesn't have a real kitchen, or he would have me in there making tamales. He called me the little senorita. This guy is unbelievable, and because he's a detective, they're letting him get away with it. I don't know what's going on with the chief, but it's like he's mesmerized by Bailey. They talk about football and hunting. It's like we've landed in a secret lair of testosterone."

"You need to lodge a complaint. This is bigotry, sexism, and an outbreak of good-old-boy disease."

Mary laughed. "I've never heard it put like that before, but you're right on all counts—Bailey has a raging case."

"So, what can you do about it?"

"Nothing. That's just the way the world is when you're a woman with brown skin who works in the police department."

She was right. Every cop show on TV consisted of white men catching criminals. Mary took things in stride. Just another reason I liked her. She was strong and smart. Smarter than Officer Jerry any day.

I leaned against the counter, crossing my arms. Thanks to Bailey's meddling, my under-the-table police investigation information on the case had been blocked. "So, I guess this means you don't have any new information on Henry Fielding's case?"

"Nope. At least when I was a glorified file clerk, I could look through the files, but now I only connect calls, which reminds me, I'd better get back. Detective Bailey's office is right around the corner. He's probably in there writing down every time I leave dispatch to do anything, even using the bathroom."

"There is one thing you can do. Officer Jerry doesn't want to straighten out the files they keep leaving on your desk. I don't think he'd turn you away if you offered to straighten them out for you."

"Is that right? That lazy jerk. Hmmm, there are so many ways I can get him in trouble by misfiling. They'd blame him."

"Sure, they would, but you have to think about the people who need their cases to see the courtroom. It wouldn't be fair to them." I reminded her.

Mary nodded in agreement. "Okay, I'll straighten out a few, but I'll see if Henry's file is in the pile."

As we started back to the dispatcher's office, I offered what I had learned through Ben and my questioning of the people around Henry. "Ben and I have been conducting our own investigation into the Henry Fielding murder. We've talked to Shep Olmstead at the marina and are sure someone has been taking boats for joyrides. One boat has a scrape on one side that could be credited to the boat thieves. Of course, we don't know that for sure."

A throat cleared from behind us in the hallway. Detective T.J. Bailey towered over us. How long had he been standing there? The man was big, both in height and stature. He had his thumbs in his belt loops, and his head was cocked to the side. The buttons on his shirt were slightly strained as they attempted to provide closure for the barrel chest underneath. His aviator-style sunglasses were turned sideways and clipped onto the collar of his shirt. I was sure there was a cowboy hat in his office to complete the look. There are few people I dislike before they've spent less than five minutes with me, but Detective Bailey got under my skin.

"You know," he said, his drawl closer to the Louisiana side of Texas than the Dallas area, "being a detective and all, I just naturally listen in to conversations around me." He turned on a smile, then raised his eyebrows, pitching his head back slightly. He did these motions so suddenly it looked like he had flicked some switch. "Did I just hear that you and someone named Ben are conducting your own investigation of Henry Fielding's death outside of the police department? Is that what you were sharing with our dispatcher?"

I didn't like the tone he was taking, and I also didn't like how he referred to Mary, a trained police officer, as the dispatcher. Mary might have had to be nice to the guy, but I didn't. "You heard right. Henry Fielding was a coworker and friend. What happened to him was terrible, and I want to know whose fault it was."

"I see. You imagine yourself as a little lady of justice." He stroked his chin. "And this 'Ben,' is that the same reporter I met at Gleason's Hardware when I attempted to interview Nelson White?"

"Yes. He's covering the story for *The Camden Courier*." I felt proud of this last part because it showed we weren't rank amateurs. Ben was an investigative reporter. A part of the media.

Bailey straightened at the word 'reporter.' "And that is all I need to hear. The Camden Police Department shares information about ongoing cases through press releases that have been approved by my office. We do not condone outside sources with cockamamie theories spreading misinformation to the public. You and your friend Ben have been warned. Stay out of our investigation, or I'll cite you for interfering in police business. Do you follow that, little girl? I can explain it again with smaller words if you like." He turned to Mary. "And as for you, I expect you to relay calls through dispatch, not leak to the press. You can bet this incident will be documented in your employment folder."

"Yes, sir." Mary said it in a small voice I hadn't heard before. This was not the Mary I knew. Where was her fire? Where was her sass?

I pulled out some of my own. "Are you kidding me? Don't talk to her like that." I protested.

"Mary is an employee of the Camden Police Department, which means she has to abide by the rules." Bailey glared at me, looking surprised I had dared to talk back during his scolding.

I didn't stop there. "I'd like to know why Mary, who trained as an officer, is now working dispatch. She used to be part of the investigative team. Why did that change?"

A patch of red spread from Bailey's full lower neck to his forehead. "Little Missy, I don't know who you think you are, but personnel matters are clearly none of your business. Not only do I not want to see you anywhere near the Fielding investigation, but I don't want to see your pretty little behind in this building. Have I made myself clear on that? Officer Jerry?" He yelled toward the front of the offices. Jerry came running like a dog on a chain.

"Yes, sir?"

"Make sure this young lady is not permitted entry into this police station. We have work to do, and she's choosing to socialize with one of our employees."

"Yes, sir!" Jerry couldn't hide his glee.

"You mean one of your officers, don't you? Or did you sweep that under the rug because my friend is a woman and not as white as your pretty little behind?"

He lifted a giant arm and pointed to the door. "Leave now!"

As I stepped around Mary, she rolled her eyes at my mention of Bailey's butt. She also gave me a tiny smile. If I had to guess, I was the first to confront the newest member of the Camden Police Department. To my surprise, a door opened further down the hall, and the chief of police stepped out.

"Everything okay, Bailey? I was on the phone with the mayor when I heard a ruckus out here." The chief looked from Bailey to Mary and then to me.

Bailey straightened and grinned. "Everything is fine. Tell the Mayor I said hello. I have it under control here."

"See that you keep it that way." The chief stepped back into his office as Bailey widened his stance.

Chapter Twelve

That night, my mother had arranged a small family gathering to celebrate my father's birthday. I was still hot under the collar from my time at the police station as I prepared my assigned side dish, green beans. How had Detective Bailey joined the Camden Police and then basically taken over the place with his sexist, racist attitudes and his condescending presence? And why was Mary, a person who treated everybody with respect regardless of skin color, putting up with his behavior? I opened the can of green beans with great fervor, pouring the green beans into a casserole dish and adding a can of cream of mushroom soup on top. I hated this recipe, and I wasn't sure anyone else liked it either, but like Mary, I was doing what I was told to do. My mother insisted on this staple.

Ben knocked on the door as I stirred with the fury of a Cat four hurricane. "It's unlocked."

He stepped in, went straight to where I was next to the kitchen counter, kissed me on the cheek, and then stepped back. "Man, I had no idea you were such a vicious cook. Those beans never had a chance. Are you upset about something?"

"I'm not mad at the green beans. I'm mad at this new detective, T.J. Bailey. The guy we met at the hardware store. What a piece of work. Did you know he had Mary demoted from police officer to dispatcher?"

Ben opened my refrigerator, scanned the empty shelves, and closed it again. "Can he do that?"

"I guess so. That's the first thing, but here's the kicker. He found out about our investigation into Henry Fielding's murder and has banned us from any kind of fact-finding activities. He won't even let me enter the police station."

Ben's eyes widened. "He what? How did that happen?"

"I guess he was mad." I hated to tell Ben about this next part. He might not have declared us enemies of the police if I had kept my opinion to myself. He might not have grown as angry as he was if I hadn't gone off on him and pointed out what a jerk he was. I would never get a job as a diplomat if I kept this up. "I guess he didn't like me telling him he was a sexist and then finished it up with calling him a good old boy."

"You said what?"

I crossed and uncrossed my arms, deciding to use my hands to make my point. "I didn't say anything that wasn't the absolute truth."

"Maybe so, but there is such a thing as tact, you know."

I dropped my head in shame. "I know," I mumbled. "But Ben, he was treating Mary like she wasn't a trained officer. He pigeonholed her as the Mexican woman who answers the phone, and it burned me up."

He reached out and slipped his hands around my waist, bringing me closer. The warmth of his body comforted me. "I guess it did. Don't think I'm not taking note of this moment; if provoked enough, my bride can really lay out a man."

I put my head on his shoulder. "I'm sorry I got you in trouble, too. The minute he figured out I was investigating on my own with my boyfriend, the reporter, I swear his head started spinning."

"It's not the first time I've gotten that reaction." He pulled away and held my hands in his. "Listen, let's go to your father's birthday party and have a good time tonight. No talking about Detective Bailey or Henry Fielding. Let's just eat cake, drink a little wine, and avoid those traumatized green beans."

As we sat around my mother's table an hour later, I already knew there was no way we'd be able to have dinner with my family and not talk about Camden's latest murder. I tried to keep it light, complimenting my mother on the balloons she had placed around the house, along with a homemade "Happy Birthday" banner. Dad's chair, the place of honor, had two red balloons attached to the back, and he was given a birthday hat that looked like a crown. It was not a look he would have wanted shared with his coworkers at the county court, but he took it all in stride. Once we sang the song, blew out the candles, and started cutting up his favorite cake, coconut, Ellie began the conversation I had hoped we would avoid.

"Any news on who killed Henry?" She caught a large bite on her fork and gulped it down, spilling a couple of crumbs. She put a hand up to her mouth. "Sorry, eating for two."

"Yes, you're eating for two, but last I checked, you're still swallowing as one," I said.

Ellie smiled through the crumbs, gulped down the ball of cake in her mouth, and said, "You wait, cousin. Someday, you'll be pregnant, and I'll be saying the same thing to you. Now tell me what you've dug up on Henry."

I glanced at Ben, then spoke. "Not much. Ben and I have been trying to figure out who had access to the boats at the marina. It seems Shep Olmstead keeps pretty busy in the afternoons."

"Doing what?" My dad asked.

I forgot my parents were sitting there. "Um, let's just say he plays a lot of jazz from the back bedroom of his house, and there is a suspicious station wagon parked out by the boats, and um…there are some interesting noises coming through the windows." Watching my parents' faces at this point was funnier than I thought it would be. My mother's eyes widened as her lips formed into a smile, and my father gave a quick nod of recognition.

"I see." He let out a cough, then continued. "With that kind of malarkey going on, stealing a boat wouldn't be that hard."

Ben agreed. "No, sir, and we think whoever has been doing this, they've done it for a while."

Ellie set down her fork. "But that still doesn't explain who is doing it. What are you going to do? Stake out the marina?"

I laughed, thinking about Ben and me sitting in his car for hours watching the marina. If Shep wasn't nervous about us finding out about his secret liaisons before, this would send him over the edge. "If we only could. We've pretty well been forbidden to do any investigating on the case."

"Why?" my mother asked.

"Because..." Ben answered. "Your daughter had it out with the new principal detective."

I quickly explained the conversation that had occurred between me and Detective Bailey.

My father grimaced. "That guy. He's been in the courthouse a few times. Don't care for him. Nobody else does either."

"Exactly," I said. "Who is this guy? And what gives him the right to be the boss of everyone suddenly?"

Ben leaned back in his chair. "You're absolutely right. Who is T.J. Bailey? Where was he before coming to Camden? Did you hear any gossip about him, Mike?" Ben asked my dad.

"Nothing. Usually, you hear a little background when someone's come from the city or a smaller town, but not him. It's like he materialized out of nowhere."

"Like a nasty rash," Ellie said under her breath, making Al rumble into a low laugh.

"You know?" Ben leaned on his chin. "If I can't investigate Henry Fielding, I might as well investigate his investigator."

I took a moment to realize what Ben was saying. "You're going to check out Detective Bailey?"

"Why not?" Ben gave a playful shrug. "He's left me with a lot of time on my hands."

I liked that idea very much, and to prove it, I kissed Ben on the cheek. He turned and kissed me back on the lips, a little longer than accepted in polite company. We were so involved I didn't hear my Aunt Mavis and Uncle Howard come into the house.

"Enough of that, you two. No public shows of affection until you tell us the date of your wedding," Mavis protested, and then she kissed my dad on the cheek. "Happy Birthday, brother." She looked at my mother. "Don't get up. I know where you stow the plates." As Uncle Howard pulled two chairs out, she went into the kitchen.

There it was again. They wanted me to set a date, and I couldn't. It was an irrational feeling, I know, but I was filled with dread trying to name a single day on the calendar. Something bad would happen. A crazy, unfounded thought, but I couldn't stop it from repeating in my mind like a ticking clock. "Soon," was all I said.

"Nope," my mother said in a tone I recognized from my childhood. "We need details. What month? What day? What hour?" She was through with my stalling. I couldn't believe she was rushing me like everyone else at the table.

Ben put a hand on my shoulder and whispered into my ear. "We need to give them a date. My parents are asking the same questions."

My mother got up and ran to the kitchen, returned shortly with her calendar from the hardware store. "Let's find a Saturday."

The words "Camden Curse" marched around in the back of my mind like a group of angry protestors. What if it was true? What if I was a curse, or worse, if I cursed the people around me? My mother put the calendar down in front of Ben and me. Ben started flipping through the pages. I took a breath and tried to quell the anxiety. I was being silly. Nothing was going to happen, and I couldn't put my life on hold just because of some crazy gossip that got back to me. Then there was that overwhelming feeling of dread.

"What do you think of an August wedding?" Ben asked gently.

"August is good," Ellie said. "The baby isn't due until September, so I'll have plenty of energy, and I have fewer brides in August. What do you think, Dot?"

Here it was. It was my moment to decide. Would I let this thing get to me and win, or would I ignore it? "August, huh?" I said, still stalling as I came to my decision. When I was a teenager, we used to go up to Ryerson's bluff, a hill that sat next to the lake. Everyone jumped off the hill into the water except me. I was sure it was unsafe and that I would break a bone or hit my head on an unseen rock. When everyone had jumped but me, I knew I couldn't get out of it. I remember holding my breath, shutting my eyes, going against the fear-based logic in my thoughts, and jumping. Here I was again on Ryerson's bluff. "August sounds good. I could do that."

"Excellent!" my mother cheered. "Now, pick which Saturday in August."

I closed my eyes and plopped a finger down on the calendar. It landed on

Friday, the thirteenth. My mother nudged my finger over a square.

"August 14th. We have a wedding day!"

Everyone around the table cheered, and it seemed nobody noticed that it wasn't the day I had actually chosen. It was an omen. Of all the days to land on, I hit Friday, the thirteenth.

Ben pulled me in for a kiss, then before he pulled away, he whispered in my ear, "It will be fine."

Could it be that he knew what I was thinking? I thought I had done well hiding my feelings from him on this. Why would I share with him I was afraid to marry him because he might be the next victim of my curse? Who would want to marry a woman with such insane thoughts about matrimony?

"All right, cousin. Now we start on the dress," Ellie said.

My mother put her hands together in front of her and started bobbing around the dining room like a squirrel who had just spotted a juicy acorn. "And we have to plan the flowers, the cake, oh, and we have to reserve the church. You'll need to do that this week, Dot."

I felt like one of those cartoon characters who had been hit on the head, but instead of stars, I was seeing white cakes and veils dancing around above me.

I took a breath as Ben reached for my hand. "It's exciting, Opal, but we don't have to do it all tonight, do we?" He quickly changed the subject. "Dot tells me you are writing a book. Is that true?"

My mother scrunched up her shoulders in glee. "I can't believe she told you." She took the bait, and relief flowed through me. "Yes, it's a mystery, but I still have so much to learn about writing." She gave him a coy smile. "But let's not get off the subject of your wedding. You're right, we have several months, but I can't wait. It'll be so much fun, won't it, Dot?"

I gave her a plastered-on smile and scrunched up my shoulders. "Fun, Mom."

Ben squeezed my hand. "I hate to change the subject of all this merriment, but Al, I was wondering if you could tell me more about Bubba Jenkins."

I was incredibly grateful he had changed the subject.

Al had been steadily eating dinner while the rest of us set a date, and he looked surprised that he'd been pulled back into the conversation. "Uh, yeah. Bubba. Bubba Jenkins. He's a groundskeeper for the city. You want me to call him?"

"That would be great," Ben said.

"He's the guy who mows the grass at the park?"

"Among other things. He plants, mows, weeds, and trims. Whatever they need him to do on city property," Al said.

I recalled a man who pushed a mower at the park. The summer I took tennis lessons, he tossed a stray tennis ball back to me. The teacher had called him Mr. Jenkins. "I didn't know his first name was Bubba."

"That's the one," Al said. "Why do you want to talk to him? Do you think he had something to do with the Fielding boy's death? You just said you were told to butt out of that murder investigation."

Ben smiled. "Detective Bailey may think he can ban me from investigating, but he'll have to catch me first."

Al gave Ben a serious look. "You do recall that this man's a detective, right?"

Ben wiggled his eyebrows. "Then I guess we'll see just how good of a detective he is, won't we?"

"You know, it's amazing that two people I haven't thought about in years have both sprung up in the last week. First Mrs. Doggett, the lunchroom lady, and now Mr. Jenkins from the park," I said.

"Oh," Ellie said, "my new assistant, Barbara, told me more about Mrs. Doggett's family. She's gone out with Chad, you know, although they aren't dating now. I guess Chad's father is absolutely driven to get both his sons in the Army and Chad isn't too excited about it."

"Wow. Army all the way." It had to be hard to go up against Big Buck Doggett.

"She also mentioned that Chad seemed to enjoy spending time with his old buddy Jeff more than he did with her. She went so far as to say that any woman who comes between those two would have to be a stunner."

My father, who had been quiet up to this point, spoke up. "That's interesting." He seemed like he was about to say something else, but then he went back to his food.

"Why is that interesting?" I asked.

"Hmm? Oh, nothing." My dad could be cagey if he thought he had something to say that might make someone uncomfortable. "Delicious cake, dear. You never disappoint."

Chapter Thirteen

On Saturday morning, a call from Ellie woke me from a sound sleep. I was dreaming I was about to walk down the aisle, but when I got to the front, there was a taped outline where Ben should have been standing. I had trouble discerning the ringing phone from the sirens in my dream. Once I pulled myself awake, I rushed to the wall phone in the kitchen.

Ellie had on her cheery morning voice. "Hey Dot. I need an enormous favor. Could you come in and work at Bluebonnets today?"

I stretched and looked at my alarm clock. 9:15. I had been planning to sleep in and enjoy my Saturday, but I knew Ellie wouldn't ask unless she had to. "I guess so."

"Thank you so much. The bride at the Doggett Wedding has put on a few, shall we say, unexpected pounds? I told her to try on the dress one last time, but she'd only put on the veil. I should have insisted, but then how could I know she was hiding the same condition I was in? They can't get the buttons to close. I wouldn't ask, except Barbara is already there helping the bridesmaids, and this is a little too advanced of an alteration for her. It should only be for an hour or so."

"I'll be there in twenty minutes." No time to perk a pot of coffee today. I'd have to hope Ellie hadn't given up coffee for the baby. She usually had a pot in the backroom near her sewing area.

"Thanks. You're a lifesaver. Say, while you're here, start going through some of my bridal magazines. Maybe you'll find something you like."

She would have to bring that up. Even though this wedding thing was making me nervous, I had to admit that it might be fun to look at the dresses. Committing to one was another matter altogether. "Be there soon."

Once I was there alone in the store, the time went by quickly. I had a bride looking through dresses, but she didn't find what she was looking for. I made her promise to come back again when Ellie was here. I looked through the spring issue of Bride's Magazine, which featured a brunette bride whose eyes were lined heavily. Her veil looked a little like a tulle umbrella that rose from the base of her head. Her dress was a white satin brocade with squared-off sleeves at the elbow, a tightly fitted bodice, and a high boat neck that extended to the shoulders. She held a bouquet of white daisies, a popular flower and not one most brides used. This woman's coloring with chestnut brown hair was the opposite of my blond reflection in the mirror, and I wasn't too sure about that umbrella veil. Looking at a few other brides, I decided I wanted my dress to be modern. No grandmother lace for me. I wanted a short skirt, and I might even shock the traditional wedding practices of Camden and wear white boots like Nancy Sinatra. I also wanted a daisy bouquet like I'd seen in the magazine. It was 1965, not 1955, and I wanted to look the part.

When Ellie came back to the store, the circles under her eyes had returned. The busy wedding season this year was taking a toll on her, and it was evident.

"How are you feeling? You don't look good."

"A little tired." She placed a hand on the small of her back. "There was a lot of bending and stitching. It's scary how easy it is for me to get tired now. The baby is still small. I can't imagine what I'll do when I'm as big as a house." She carried a large sewing box in the other hand. Like a doctor carrying a bag full of medicines to administer to a patient on a house call, her medicine bag contained pins, needles, scissors, binding tape, and thread. She was ready for anything. She even carried some aspirin and tissues in case of emotional breakdowns in the wedding party.

"Let me help. You put your feet up and let me handle the store." I took the heavy sewing basket from her. How could extra thread be so heavy?

"Don't be silly."

"I think you're the one who can be silly. Don't forget the day you took off on a bus out of town to join the Peace Corps. You about killed Al with that adventure." After we found ourselves front row and center for the J.F.K. assassination, Ellie decided she had to help the world become a better place by joining the Peace Corps. It was a great idea, but hardly realistic for her, being a woman running a small business. We were all happy to see her return, especially Al.

Ellie kicked off her shoes. "I guess I did. The bigger I get, the easier it will be for me to let somebody else in here." She waved her hand to indicate her kingdom. The Blue Bonnet's Dress Shop.

"You hired Barbara. That wasn't so bad."

Ellie returned to her folding chair. "I did, didn't I? I really like her. She helped me with the bride's dress. I also found out some big news about the groom's brother, Chad."

"Besides the fact he's going to be an uncle. Really. Do tell."

"Even though his dad is crazy for him to go into the Army, he didn't pass the physical exam. They denied him."

"What part of the physical did he fail? He looks healthy to me."

"I'm not sure, but Barbara said he showed her a form saying he did not qualify to serve."

"That's weird."

"Yeah, and his parents found out while she was there and within hearing distance. It wasn't pretty. You know his dad marches in the Veterans Day parade every year, and Al says he's a regular down at the V.F.W. Hall."

I remembered meeting him at Big Buck's Ford. He was a driven man when he wanted something. Ben didn't have a chance the minute he stepped foot in the car lot. "What did his parents say?" I asked.

A customer came in before Ellie could answer. "Welcome to Bluebonnets." She said this from her chair. She turned to me and said, "I don't know. I'm sure his dad was upset."

I thought about how every time I had seen Chad, he seemed in pursuit of a good time. I knew going into the Army was his father's plan, not his, and I wondered what he wanted to do with his life. He was a few years younger than I was, but like other young men I knew, he lacked direction. He faced life like a rich playboy. Unfortunately, he was the son of the lunch lady, and his lifestyle wasn't based on an inheritance.

I also thought about the way Henry acted with him at the fair and the funeral of Betty Weaver. As long as I'd known Henry, the only friend he had in the world was Nelson. Yet, he acted like he and Chad were friends. Buddies. Pals. With all the teasing that Chad and Jeff did, I just didn't see Henry as someone they would want to hang around with.

Ellie chuckled to herself. "Well, I guess you can't have a wedding without a little drama. First, the bride's dress didn't fit because of a sudden weight gain, and then the groom's brother announced the Army rejected him. I live for this business." If she ever wrote a book about her life around the world of white satin, it would be a bestseller.

Our lone customer left the rack she had been looking through and started for the door.

"Thanks, come again," Ellie said after her.

I picked up our conversation where Ellie left off. "Quite an interesting wedding."

Ellie gave me a sly little smile. "I'm sure your wedding day will be just as interesting."

If the Curse of Camden hit, people would never stop talking about my wedding. Talk about wedding drama. I tried to push the thought aside and picked up one of Ellie's bridal catalogs. "What would you say if I went modern with the wedding dress?"

Ellie's eyes widened, and her jaw dropped. "Just how modern?"

"How about a Twiggy look?" Twiggy was a London fashion model that everyone was crazy about because she had big eyelashes and short skirts. I wasn't as thin as she was, but I was sure I could pull off one of her miniskirts.

"I don't know, Dot." Ellie closed her lips as she thought for a moment and then said. "What will your mother say when she sees it?"

"At this point, I think my mother would be happy if I went down the aisle in a potato sack. I've been putting the wedding planning off, and I know she's frustrated."

"I'm glad you're the one who brought it up." Ellie's laugh turned into a little snort. "You're driving us all crazy, including Ben. Are you sure about this?"

"About what?"

"Getting married. Ben is a wonderful guy, but lately, you've seemed a little, I don't know, less than excited about the wedding."

I closed the catalog. "Ben is perfect, and I can't wait to be his wife. It's just that, in the last few years, I've had this swirl of activity around me."

Ellie looked confused. "What kind of swirl? Like an ice cream swirl? Ooh, that sounds delicious."

"You know. People playing out their darkest wishes and trying to get away with it. Murders, accomplices, and bodies are popping up everywhere. You know, a swirl."

"Coming from the girl who just got hired to work around dead people." Ellie stretched in her chair to ease back pain. That was when she looked at me. "Dot? What are you saying? Is that the reason? Are you worried about something happening? Something murderous?"

She had to think I was crazy, silly, stupid, and all those things. She'd dealt with plenty of nervous brides, but I was the first one worried about someone getting killed. "Think about it, Ellie. If these things keep happening in my jobs, what's to say they won't happen at my wedding? What if something happened to Ben, to you, or anyone else I loved? I can't let that happen."

Ellie pulled herself out of the chair and immediately drew me into a hug. "Oh, Dot, I'm so sorry you've been feeling like this."

"I'm the Camden Curse. Everyone is right."

She held me tighter. "No, you're not, and if I find out who started saying that, I will personally knock 'em to the moon. We live in Texas. We love sending people to the moon. Please don't do this to yourself."

I stepped back. "Thank you for pledging to knock out whoever started this ugly rumor, but you have to admit, there is an element of truth to it. Henry was a sweet kid who just wanted a nice car and a girlfriend. His father adored him and would have done anything for him. Now Henry's gone, and his father will never be the same. This is the kind of damage I do to people."

Ellie reached over the counter for a tissue, a necessary tool when working with brides and their mothers. She placed it in my hand. "No. No. No. You need to reroute that thinking. Ben will be fine. We'll be fine, but giving up

88

your happiness because of your past is just not a smart thing to do. I love you, cousin, but sometimes you get some nutty things in your head."

"But—"

"No buts. Promise me you will go forward with your life and not let someone else's words govern you."

I blew my nose. "Okay."

"Say it."

"I promise to go forward and ignore what people are saying."

Chapter Fourteen

On Sunday afternoon, Ben and I drove over to Laughton Funeral Home for Henry's funeral. It was strange being in a funeral home other than Fielding, but strangely familiar seeing Oliver sitting in the front row with his mother, Neva, Dina, Arnie, and Nelson White. Further down the pew sat a woman I presumed was Henry's mother and her husband. She was a small, thin woman wearing a hat with a black lace veil. Her shoulders shook as she pulled a handkerchief up under the veil. After one particularly loud sniff, Neva shot her with a disapproving look. After she shared her opinion of the ex-wife with me that day, I was never sure if she was unhappy with her because she left Henry or because of her disdain for the family business. Many times, Neva stressed the importance of the continuation of the funeral home after the death of Oliver's father.

Chad and Jeff were sitting near the back, whispering to each other. Mrs. Doggett sat on the other side. Big Buck Doggett wasn't in attendance, the same as Betty Weaver's funeral. It was interesting Chad was not sitting with his mother. No doubt, they were still on the outs after his big revelation at the wedding.

As the organ music started, more people filtered into the small funeral service room. One of the funeral attendants was quietly closing the door when Detective Bailey squeezed by him and took a seat in the back next to Margaret.

He glanced around the room, no doubt looking for someone to arrest, when his gaze lit on me. His eyes were like little black bees about to shoot out of his head. My father always told me the best thing you can do with a bully is throw them off balance, so I tilted my head to the side, smiled and bobbed my fingers in a wave. I'm sure the dogged detective expected me to slink away after being caught directly disobeying his orders by being in his very presence. It wasn't a crime to attend the funeral of a friend and coworker, so I didn't care what he thought.

After my wave, he grunted, took off his cowboy hat, and sat in the back row, settling his head into his double chin.

The funeral itself was simple, with a Presbyterian minister walking us through the service. Henry's casket was open, and his head was raised for the attendees to see him throughout the service. Thankfully, this time, the boat had not caused disfigurement to Henry's face, as it had to Betty Weaver's. It was strange to see him lying there when he had been so full of life last week. Whoever did this to him needed to be caught. From the paleness of Henry's face to the shudders in his father's shoulders, the sadness and anger burned within my chest. Someone needed to pay for what they'd done. Unfortunately, the detective in charge was more about putting people in their place than solving crimes. I invited Mary to come with me today, but she begged off. She must have known Bailey would attend the funeral and was avoiding the new detective. He had done enough to damage her career.

When the final hymn was sung, and they wheeled Henry out, Ben and I moved to the aisle to leave.

Ben whispered in my ear. "Well? Do you see a murderer in this room?"

"Dot?" Mrs. Doggett came up behind Ben. "Here we are again at another funeral. I remember Henry from the lunch line. Such a nice young man."

Of course, she remembered, but did she also remember or even realize how much her son, Chad, bullied him? "We do seem to be meeting at funerals a lot lately, don't we? You are very sweet to come here for him."

Mrs. Doggett put her hand on her heart. "Of course, I'd come. I will never forget my kids, even when they're grown."

"That's very good of you. Not everyone remembers us years after high school." I changed the subject as we neared the door behind the crowd. "I hear you had a wedding in your family yesterday."

"We did. My Stevie is married. I can't believe it. I guess it's just a matter of time before Chad finds a girl and settles down."

I smiled, wondering how she felt about Chad. He wasn't following his father's wishes and as far as the girl went, Barbara had told us it was hard to come between him and Jeff. Still, I played along. "Sure. I guess it happens to all of us."

"Even you." She touched my hand and gave me a knowing smile. "Congratulations on your engagement."

"Thank you."

Ben echoed me. "Thank you."

Her gaze took in Ben. She inquired politely. "When is the wedding?"

"We just set a date," he answered. "August 14th." The way he said it was so relaxed. Between the flowers, the dress, the venue, and everything else that was making me doubt my sanity for the next few months, the best I could have done was to choke the words out.

"Wonderful. I'll be looking for my invitation," Mrs. Doggett said as we went through the door.

Oliver was at the back of the church, talking to the mourners. We waited in line. I inevitably noticed that Dina White stood next to him and occasionally reached down and squeezed his hand. He would give her a gentle smile and move on to the next well-wisher. Arnie was sitting within Dina's sight, reading the latest issue of *The Green Lantern*, where yet another villain had a plot to conquer the universe.

When we reached Oliver, my emotions overwhelmed me, and I hugged him before speaking. Finally, I whispered, "I'm so sorry, Oliver."

"I know. I'm just working on getting through this day." He glanced at Dina and then back to me.

My eyes drifted to Dina. Because of Nelson she had spent years around Henry. Losing him had to be tough on her as well. "I'm also sorry for your loss," I said softly in Dina's direction. She looked confused at my words. "It's just that he and Nelson were so close. It has to be hitting you as well."

She took my hand and held it in hers. "That is very kind of you to say. We all spent time together. Two little one-parent families. It was so sad the boys were having a disagreement when Henry died. Nelson told me he thought they were getting closer to solving their problem, but Henry canceled at the last minute. Now, we all wish we had known more about what was going on in that boy's head."

"How is Nelson doing?" I asked.

"As good as can be expected." She whispered, her eyes searching out her son in the room. "It's going to take time."

Once we made it outside, the crowd dispersed to their cars, some going to the cemetery and some going home. Chad was leaning up against a tree, smoking a cigarette, and Jeff stood next to him, hands in his pockets. Chad looked like a scene out of Rebel Without a Cause. He carried off that James Dean "cool look" like he was the teen idol himself.

Ben was walking to his new car, but I touched his arm. "Give me a minute, will you?"

He looked over at the boys. "Sure. You want me to go with you?"

"No. This shouldn't take too long." As I walked over, I tried to think of ways to steer the conversation toward Chad's Army rejection. "Chad. Nice to see you again, even though it's at another funeral."

"It can't be helped. People live. People die." He said it flatly as he took in a drag of his cigarette.

"So, your girlfriend is working at my cousin's shop."

Jeff wrinkled his forehead, looking confused. "What girlfriend? I didn't know you had a girlfriend."

"Who is that?" Chad still looked confused and then scowled.

"Barbara. It sounds like it was fortunate she was there with some last-minute fittings."

"Oh, her. I wouldn't say she's my girlfriend. We had some fun, a couple of dates, but that was it. I was with another girl at the wedding, not that she's my girlfriend either. Doesn't look good to go to a family wedding without a chick on your arm."

The way he put it, having a girl with him did not differ from choosing the right outfit. It was about how it looked and contained no emotional value. "You know, Barbara told me something interesting about you," I said.

Chad stood up, hoisting his body away from the tree. "What would that be?"

"She said you were rejected when you tried to join the service. That must have been an awful disappointment for you. Why did they reject you?"

Chad rubbed his hands on the front of his pants. "She told you all that?"

"Oh, yes," I said. "She overheard it, I guess."

"Not that it's any of your business, but I had a physical reason why I was rejected. Before you try to ask what, just know I don't particularly want to share something that will end up being gossip in this town."

He didn't look happy I had brought this up. I played it off by putting my hand to my mouth and then drew closer. "Oh, okay. I see."

"It's nothing bad. Just know I tried, and they wouldn't take me. No big deal."

"I'll bet your dad thought it was a big deal," I said.

"I don't care what my old man thinks." He threw down his cigarette and mushed it with his foot. "As much as I've loved talking with you, Dot, I need a drink."

Jeff came closer, leaning over, putting his face close to mine. "You know, for such a good-looking girl, you sure are nosy. Looks only go so far with me, which could lead to trouble if you can't mind your business."

He rejoined Chad, and as they walked away, I realized that, along with the smoke, I smelled liquor on Chad's breath. Was there ever a day when he wasn't drinking? There was something not right here, and I wanted to know more. The recruitment office was right across from the hardware store. Maybe I'd stop by and see what I could find out about Chad Doggett's rejection from the Army.

Before I could rejoin Ben, I realized there was another source of smoke coming my way. It wasn't cigarette smoke, but a cigar. Leaning up against a dark blue Ford Galaxy, T.J. Bailey had been watching the entire conversation. When my eyes met his, he tilted his head, smiled, and waved.

Chapter Fifteen

I made it back to work on Tuesday, where Oliver's new assistant, Peter, greeted me. He was as young as I was and just out of mortuary school. He wore a crisp black suit, no doubt a gift for his graduation. He had rusty brown hair with a slight curl on the top and filled out his suit at the waist. He extended a pudgy hand.

"How do you do? I'm Peter. I hope you don't mind, but I needed to pack Henry's things. I know it seems sudden," he said as he added some of Henry's items to a box.

"No, that's fine. You need to set up your own work area." Henry's office looked empty. All reminders of him were disappearing. It was like he never inhabited Fielding Funeral Home. The spare bottles of embalming fluid stock were still on the walls, along with a small library of books on the science of embalming. The smell of formaldehyde hung in the air. "Sorry we didn't get this cleaned up for you."

He handed me the box he had been packing. "Don't worry about it. It gave me the chance to know a little about Oliver's son. He told me about the accident. Such a tragedy." He looked around the room. "I'll try to do right by him and his father. You may not have guessed, but this is my first job as a mortician."

I feigned surprise. "Really?"

"Oh yes, and here, on my first day, we are already expecting a body from the nursing home." He pressed his palms together in, I hate to say it, excitement.

"Well, then, I'll take the box, and you'd better get to work. Nice to meet you."

Glad to be out of that level of the funeral home, I escaped back to my desk in the lobby. Putting Henry's box on my desk—the few items that were there—made me sad. A couple of car magazines with buxom women sitting on the hood. A pack of Pall Malls.

I didn't even know Henry smoked. At the bottom of the box, underneath the pack of cigarettes, was a matchbook. Not any matchbook, but one with Uncle Sam on the cover. In his typical blue Serge jacket, white shirt, and red bow tie, he stared at me from under his white top hat, with the star in the middle next to him. "Today's Army wants to join you."

I turned the matchbook over to the other side. Written in red and blue lettering on a white background, there were the words *Over 300 matchless opportunities guaranteed in writing before you enlisted.*

When I opened the matchbook, there was even more written there in tiny type.

Check out these enlistment options. 16 months guaranteed in Europe, Hawaii, Panama, or Alaska

Guaranteed stateside unit of choice

One hundred and twenty-day delayed entry program

Schools

A soldier could go from combat to working in the kitchen or doing payroll. It was quite an excellent sales tool for recruiters, but I wanted to know where Henry had picked up this thing. It proved that he visited an Army recruiter, and I had to ask if this was the afternoon when Henry disappeared with the hearse. This proved just how unhappy Henry was working at the mortuary. It was ironic Henry was getting sucked in by this advertising while Chad only went there because his father insisted. Who knew? Maybe Henry would have found happiness serving his country. I needed to go to the recruiter's office across the street from the hardware store. If there was some paperwork with Henry's name on it, he could track it down for me. Unfortunately, I had work to do today, but when Oliver asked me to go to the office supply store to pick up some new typewriter ribbons, I gladly agreed. I wanted to take Mary with me, but there was a chance this time she would lose her job instead of getting demoted if she got involved with what I was doing.

When it came time for me to get the office supplies, I made a quick stop and parked my car in front of the Army recruiter's office. In the windows were pictures of soldiers going into action somewhere, looking brave and wearing Hollywood smiles. When I opened the door, a man sitting in a khaki uniform with a short, buzz haircut looked up and smiled.

"Well, hello there, miss. It's been a slow morning, and I certainly didn't expect to see a beautiful girl come in the door." He had the air of someone who flirted easily with young women. I met guys like this all the time, and I wasn't above flirting back to get my information.

"Good afternoon." I stepped closer. "I need to ask you a favor."

"Don't tell me; let me guess. You want to go into the Army? Is that it?"

"Not exactly. I had a friend that I think might have come in to enlist in the Army. He passed away last week."

The recruiter's expression changed. "I'm sorry to hear that, ma'am."

"Thank you. I found this matchbook." I held it up for him to see. "I found this in his belongings, and I was wondering if he stopped by your office to talk about enlisting."

"He could have. What did he look like? What was his name?"

"His name was Henry Fielding. He was about 5'9, weighed 130 pounds, and had brown hair. Soft-spoken. Oh, and one more thing." I tried to slip the next part into the conversation casually. "He might have been driving a hearse."

The recruiter, who had been nodding at my description, paused. "Really? Driving a hearse?"

"Yes. His father is a mortician. He disappeared with the hearse one afternoon, and I'm wondering if this is where he went."

"Well, there wasn't a hearse out front, or I would have remembered that. Let me just see who enlisted last week to see if we have anything that sounds like him. You say his name was Henry Fielding?"

"Yes."

The recruiter put his hand on his chin and then went to a filing cabinet and rifled through the files.

After a minute of searching, he came up with an empty look. "I don't see anybody named Henry here."

"Could you see if he went to a different office?"

"I'd have to track it down. We turn in our reports once a week, so that would be at the central office. So sorry for your loss, ma'am. It's a sad thing when a man decides to serve his country but doesn't make it too basic. Even if he works for a funeral home, sadly, the Army needs those guys, too."

I thanked the recruiter and went back out to my car. Nelson was across the street, sweeping the sidewalk in front of the hardware store. I waved, but he looked down.

That afternoon, as I changed out Oliver's typewriter ribbon, I thought about when I could find time to visit the recruiting office in Dallas. Now that the funeral home had reopened, I only had my lunch breaks to investigate, so it would be difficult. I had paper jammed in my typewriter and was trying to extract it when a familiar voice came through the door.

"Excuse me, miss, but is it true a mortician will be the last to let you down?" Mary stood at Oliver's office door.

I laughed. "Yes, I suppose you're right. What are you doing here? I thought you were busy dispatching cops to find lost puppies."

"If you only knew how right you were. No." She looked around the front lobby. "I thought I should visit your new job, although I have visited this funeral home before."

I was happy to see Mary, but her explanation for being here sounded weak. "Come on out to where my desk is, and we can talk. How long have you got?"

Mary shook her head and let out a breath. "Oh, I'm yours for as long as you can stand me."

This did not sound good. "Mary? Did you lose your job?"

"No, not yet, but Detective Bailey decided it was slow at the station, so he talked the chief into sending me home for the afternoon."

Why was it every time she mentioned Detective Bailey's name, something bad happened to her? "Can he do that?" I asked.

"I guess so, because here I am."

"That guy's trouble. You know, Ben said he was going to check on him. I know it's tough working with all men, but this man has it out for you."

"Nothing gets by Detective Dot Morgan. You know he was angry when he saw you at the funeral. I heard him complaining about seeing you there. I don't think he remembered your connection to the victim. Which reminds me. I volunteered to help Jerry out with the files."

I knew it would work. I was feeling pretty good about my plan for her to infiltrate the investigation even though the men in the office kept demoting her. "And?"

"They don't have much. They're spending all their time questioning his friend Nelson."

"I don't think he has it in him to murder his best friend."

"Yeah, well, they do."

I thought of his mother, Dina. It would devastate her if her son was sent to prison for a crime he didn't do. "They haven't questioned anyone else?"

"His father, but he's been cleared. Oh, and I looked at the crime scene photos, but you actually saw the crime scene, so nothing new there. I will say there sure was a lot of trash on shore. Beer bottles, gum wrappers, pop tops."

"That's the way the lake is all the time. Nothing new there."

Mary looked around. "I hate to say it, but this place is dead today. Where is everybody?"

In the years I had known Mary, I never realized she had this dark sense of humor regarding funeral homes. "They are downstairs. Oliver hired a guy to replace Henry, and he's been training him for most of the day."

"Good." Mary sniffed one of the flower arrangements. "So, now it's my turn. What have you come up with in the Henry Fielding case?"

Yay. Mary was here. I had been wanting to talk to her all day but didn't want to chance going to the station. "Some interesting stuff. I went through a box of Henry's things and found a pack of matches from the Army recruiter's office. I think Henry might have tried to enlist."

"Did you ask his father?"

"Yes, but he knew nothing about it."

"You know, Carlos has already reported to Basic at Fort Leonard Wood. He broke our mother's heart, but he keeps telling her he can have an actual career there. He kept telling her about all of the career opportunities the

Army was offering him and she was actually starting to buy it."

"Did he mention his home office could end up being on the firing line in Vietnam?"

"No, but it has to be on his mind. I hoped they wouldn't take him because of a physical flaw like flat feet, but no, they couldn't wait to get their hands on him."

The words "physical flaw" rang in my head. I forgot there were certain things the Army would reject in an applicant. Henry had a physical flaw. "Hey Mary, would you reject an applicant on the police force for a hearing loss?"

"Sure. He wouldn't be safe in combat. The fire department would flag it, too."

"So, if Henry tried to enlist, they would reject him. I don't know if you knew this, but he couldn't hear out of one ear."

"You're right. I didn't know that about him, but what would this have to do with his death? It might keep him out of the Army, but I've never heard of somebody getting killed because they have a hearing loss."

"I'm not sure, but I have an idea."

Oliver came into the lobby from downstairs. His gaze lit on Mary. "Can I help you? I didn't know we had anyone up here." He took in her uniform. "Do you have any information on my son's case? Did they find his killer?"

Mary shook her head. I knew my friend, and I knew it killed her not to tell him what he needed to hear. "No. Sorry. I'm a friend of Dot's. I'm not assigned to his case, but you can bet they are working hard to find out, sir."

"Thank you for saying that, ma'am. I don't want to sound ungrateful, but the new detective in charge seemed terribly busy and not very approachable. Being a mortician, it's my business to read people, and I wasn't sure if my son's case was all that important to him."

"Every murder victim is important, Mr. Fielding," Mary said. "Especially somebody's child. Frankly, I don't know how you stay calm. I'd be a mess. I have children of my own."

Oliver's eyes were red on the lower rims. " Inside, I'm falling apart, but I have a business to run. Thank you for saying that. Could I ask you a favor?"

Mary's face softened. "Anything, Mr. Fielding."

"Call me Oliver. Would you be willing to help me ask questions when I need to? Be my liaison with Detective Bailey?"

Oliver assumed Bailey would actually listen to Mary. "I'm not sure I'm the right person to ask, Oliver. I get under his skin."

Oliver straightened. "In my opinion, that makes you the best person for the job."

She nodded. "Then I'd be glad to help any way I can."

"And what was your name, Officer?" Oliver asked.

"Mary Oliva."

"It's nice to meet you, Mary."

"Mr. Fielding," Peter called from downstairs.

"I'll be right there." Oliver returned the way he came in.

"You have a great boss. It is awful he lost his boy the way he did."

"Which is why we have to find out who killed him."

"And you think it has to do with that matchbook, I suppose?"

"Sure do. Want to come with me after work to pay a call to somebody?"

"I'm not sure if I like that look in your eyes, so, yes, count me in. You're dangerous when you're on your own."

Mary was doing more than just supporting a friend. Her job was at stake if she got caught helping me investigate Henry's murder. "Are you sure you want to do this?"

"What do I have to lose?"

My office intercom buzzed. "Dot," Neva. said. If you are all caught up, you can leave early today. We're still getting back on our feet, and I have nothing else for you to do. We need to cut expenses after taking those days off."

"Okay, if you're sure."

"It's a beautiful afternoon. Enjoy the rest of your day."

After Neva closed out the intercom, Mary gave me a mischievous look. "You know what that means?"

I pulled my purse out of the bottom drawer of my desk and grabbed my sweater. "Watch out Camden, here we come?"

"You bet. Let's do it." She turned back. "Where are we headed?"

"To find Chad Doggett, I need to ask him a question. "

"Big Buck Doggett's kid? Why?" Mary asked as we left the funeral home. "Why would you want to talk to him?"

"Because I think he can tell us why Henry had a pack of matches from the recruiter's office. He works at his father's car lot."

Mary climbed into my car, putting her purse on her lap. "I don't think so. My kids told me the janitor at the school has a new helper. It's the lunch lady's son."

"No. Ben just bought a new car, and Chad was working there."

"Then he's also working at the school. Let's go find out." When Mary said it, him working at the school made sense. If he was no longer going into the service, his father would want him to work somewhere, and maybe he didn't want to see his son working beside him at the car lot. Chad struck me as a man who would depend on his mother in any crisis. It would be easy for him to get a quick job.

When we entered Camden School, a complex that housed kids from kindergarten to senior year, the familiar smells of cafeteria food, paste, and children fresh from recess hung in the air.

"Should we check in at the office?" I asked.

Mary frowned. "I don't know if that's a good idea. I'm afraid the principal will catch sight of my uniform and think Chad is in trouble. Let's see if we can find him on our own first."

She was right about the uniform. As we walked past various classroom doors, the students would look our way, waiting to see if we were coming to break up a boring afternoon. We found Chad folding up tables in the cafeteria.

"There he is," Mary said. Luckily, the cafeteria was empty, and the only other people I saw were the lunchroom staff cleaning up for the day.

"Hey Chad," I walked over to where he was pushing a table to its storage space on the wall.

Instead of the jeans and striped shirts he usually wore, today he wore workman's overalls. Dressed in the garb of a janitor, he looked somehow older. A slight odor of alcohol hung around him. Every time I talked to him in the last few weeks, he had been drinking, and from the smell that seemed to come out of his pores, he had taken a drink today as well. Even though Chad was my age, I concluded he was a heavy drinker to the point of being an alcoholic.

"What are you doing here?" He asked.

"Looking for you," I answered.

Chad scowled as his gaze lit on Mary. "You brought a cop with you? Are you following me? You are one weird chick. What's this all about?"

"Dot?" Margaret Doggett came out of the kitchen, hairnet on, wiping her hands on her apron. "This is a surprise."

I hadn't been counting on letting Mrs. Doggett hear what I had to say and considered trying to do it at another time.

"Is there something wrong?" She gestured to Mary.

"No, ma'am," Mary quickly inserted. "I'm here as a friend of Dot's. I'm not here to arrest anybody, unless you think I should." Mary tried to make light of it, and it took a moment for Mrs. Doggett to realize that.

"Oh, I see. I jumped to conclusions. You were talking to Chad, and, well, you know. A mother worries." When she smiled, an extra set of wrinkles settled around her eyes. She was such a sweet lady. It seemed impossible she gave birth to a character like Chad. What happened there to cause him to act the way he did?

"So," Chad said. "What's this all about? I know you like me, but I didn't expect you to track me down at my new job." His mood switched from anger to mild flirting when his mother joined us.

"How long have you been working at the school?" I asked.

"Just a day or two. My old man said that because I couldn't qualify to go to Vietnam, I had to get a job in Camden or leave. Yes, I'm not good enough for the old man's car lot."

Margaret stepped forward and said, "And Mr. Miller has been looking for an assistant janitor for the longest time. I love having my boy on the job."

Chad sneered. "If you say so."

"I'm still curious about you not qualifying for active duty. You seem like a strong guy who could take on anything or anyone. Can I ask why they rejected your application?"

"Uh." He rubbed his chin and looked at the floor. "Well, it's kind of personal, you know."

As he pleaded for privacy, I suspected he was thinking something up.

I leaned forward. "How's your hearing, by the way?"

Mrs. Doggett laughed. "His hearing? Chad hears just fine."

I pulled out the pack of matches. "Funny thing about these matches. I found them in a box of Henry Fielding's things. You wouldn't know anything about these, would you?"

"No," he answered dryly. "Why would I care what you found in Henry's stuff? I barely knew the guy."

I had him. He hadn't been around Henry enough to see the change in him or how excited he was to see him and Jeff at the funeral. "He knew you. He acted like you wanted to be his friend, which I found confusing because when we were all in school together, you were the opposite of Henry's friend. You bullied him. You and Jeff. You teased him because he was deaf in one ear, didn't you?"

"I beg your pardon." Margaret cut in as anger crept into her voice. "My boy would never bully anyone. He knows better than that."

Margaret Doggett was in the dark about her son. If she only knew how much of a bully he was, she wouldn't be so proud to have him at her job every day.

"How much did you pay him?" Mary asked.

Henry shook his head in a fast motion. "I don't know what you're talking about. Why would I pay him? That guy was nothing but a loser. It's pitiful that he thinks I was his friend."

"Didn't your mother just say that you weren't a bully? You sure sound like a bully to me." I said.

Mrs. Doggett dried her hands on her apron and then put her arm through her son's. "Really, Dot. Whatever high you are on, the things you are saying are hurtful. You young people."

What was it with the older generation? They always assumed someone had to be on drugs if they didn't behave in the way they thought they should. Did she not notice I was standing there with a cop? Did she think we were out in the parking lot smoking a joint together? "Mrs. Doggett, when was the rejection slip from the recruiter's office dated? Do you remember?"

"I don't know," she said, putting a work-reddened hand on her neck. "Maybe a week or two before the wedding. Chad said he didn't want to spoil the family's special day. He's considerate like that."

"Isn't he, though?" Mary snorted.

"If I had to guess, I'll bet it was the same day that Henry Fielding disappeared for two hours with the hearse."

Chad laughed. "Henry stole the hearse. Are you kidding me?"

"He was supposed to be gassing it up, for your information." Even though Henry had tricked the government, I would not make fun of him now. "Mrs. Doggett, did you catch where the recruitment office was that your son was rejected at?"

"Yes." She looked at her son. "It was an office in Dallas."

I turned to Chad. "We have a perfectly good recruitment office right here in town, Chad. Right across the street from the hardware store. Why would you go out of town like that?"

"Yeah, why?" Mary echoed.

Margaret put a hand on her son's shoulder. "I was curious about that as well and asked Chad about it. He didn't want the whole town to know. That's all. If he had gone to the office in town, Sargent Smith knows his father. I think if he had gone to him, he might not have been turned away."

"And then your darling boy, Chad, would be on his way to basic training at Fort Leonard Wood, wouldn't he?" I asked.

"Yes, but I guess it wasn't to be." Margaret believed the lies her son had told her.

"Mrs. Doggett, did you know Henry suddenly had a big wad of cash right after his trip out with the hearse?"

"That's nice."

"Yes, and I think if we counted it, we'd find the exact amount you saved for your dress at Bluebonnets." After I said the last few words, Chad decided he had to get back to work. He went to the next table and started folding in the seats.

"Chad?" Margaret asked. "What is she trying to tell me? Did you take my money and give it to Henry Fielding?"

"No." He yelled, his voice echoing in the empty cafeteria. "Why would I do something like that?"

"I'll tell you why," Mary said, looking excited. She'd figured it out. "Because you paid Henry to go in and give your name to the recruiter. When he told him he couldn't hear out of one ear and wasn't a candidate, he had the sergeant write him a rejection letter. He gave it to you, and you gave him the cash."

"What? I'd never do anything as stupid as that."

"You would," I said, "if you didn't want to go fight in Vietnam and had no other way out."

He turned to his mother. "Don't listen to them, Mom. She thinks she's some kind of detective. Did you know they call her The Curse of Camden? It's because people die around her. She's bad luck."

Margaret stood quietly, looking at her son. She didn't smile. She didn't cry. She looked at him as if she were seeing him for the first time.

"Don't believe her, Mom." Chad tried to pull her back and put his hand on her rounded shoulder.

She removed his hand and walked back into the kitchen.

Chad turned, a raging anger in his eyes. "You bitch. Why did you have to tell her?"

I put the matchbook back in my pocket. "And why do I think that Henry enlisting for you is just the tip of the iceberg?" I knew where I needed to go next.

Chad stepped so close to me I could smell stale beer on his breath. "You need to stay out of my business. Have you ever thought the curse could apply to you, too?"

"Is that a threat?" Mary asked.

Chad held a hand up in the air. "I'm an innocent man, Officer. I was just reminding Dot of that. That's all."

Chapter Sixteen

After leaving the school with our newly found facts about Henry Fielding's death, Mary and I marched into the police station full of purpose. We walked in step, the rhythm of our feet in sync. The closer we got to Detective Bailey's office, the weaker our steps became. Images of Bailey bounced around in my mind, none of them welcoming. He would hate this, especially coming from us. What were we but two interfering women, one of us, not even a police officer? This could be a terrible idea.

"Are you sure he'll be open to listening to us?" I asked.

Mary gave a little snort through her nose. "No. He won't. He hates the idea of women in the police force, especially women like me. But if he's a good detective, he'll at least listen to us."

The detective part was right, but I had trouble with the last part. "If you say so."

She placed her hand on my arm. "It's all we've got. Just remember. We're doing this for Henry."

I kept repeating that phrase in my mind as we approached Bailey's desk. He hunched over an open file, a cigarette burning in a white metal ashtray next to him. He ran his finger along a typed line, as if trying to absorb whatever he was reading into his brain through his fingerprint. Mary cleared her throat, and his gaze went from Mary to me. That's when the scowl came over his features. He didn't look like a man ready to listen to us, even if we could hand him Henry's killer on a silver platter.

"I thought I banned you from setting foot in this station."

His voice, his posture, and his condescension set me off. This was for

Henry, and I would not let this oaf treat me like a jaywalker. "Officer Jerry must have been on a bathroom break because I walked right in. Then again, if you are counting on Jerry to do anything more than meet and greet at the front desk, you're out of luck. You know men, so flighty." His little black eyes hardened. I had hit a nerve.

Mary spoke, picking up my attitude. "We're here because we stumbled onto some information relevant to the Henry Fielding case."

He sat back in his chair and steepled his fingers in front. At first, he smiled and let out a little chuckle. "You found a clue, huh, Sherlock?"

I didn't like his tone or the way he was looking at us. He wasn't listening to us. It felt like he was trying to remember everything we said so he could tell the guys later over a beer. *Hey, fellas, guess what these two dames tried to do today?*

"Listen," I said a little sharply. "I think Henry Fielding faked joining the Army using someone else's name. Someone who didn't want to go to Vietnam. He had a large amount of cash that came from nowhere, and I have evidence he was at a recruiter's office."

He slanted his eyebrows, making his eyes look even smaller. "What's that got to do with the price of eggs?"

I hated that saying. "The person he enlisted for had a motive to kill him."

"And I suppose you know who this person is?" Bailey asked, shifting to the desk and picking up a pen and paper.

"Chad Doggett."

He put the pen back down. He tipped his head forward as if he hadn't heard right. "Doggett? As in Big Buck Doggett's son?"

"Do you know him?" I asked. Bailey hadn't been in town that long, so unless he'd bought a car, the chances of him knowing him were amazing.

"I've seen him down at the V.F.W. I can already tell you any son of Buck Doggett would not let some namby pamby fake enlist for him. You've got the wrong man, but then, of course, you two don't know what the hell you're doing. Isn't there a Tupperware party you could go to or something? Because you're wasting my time here."

Mary crossed her arms. "And that's it? You're the judge and jury? You decided he's innocent, so that's all there is to it? Where were you before this job? Did they let you run roughshod over everything there and ignore any true investigative techniques? Is that why you're in a small town like Camden?"

I tried to pull Mary back away from Bailey. She had been so cool and respectful to her bully boss, but now she was like a kettle letting off steam.

Bailey stood up, asserting his physical size over Mary, who was small in comparison. "Beg your pardon, Officer? Are you questioning my command? Because if you do, I'll be forced to write you up for insubordination."

"Go ahead, and while you're filling out the paperwork, I'm going to take what we've uncovered to the chief. He needs to know what a piss-poor job you're doing here." There was no stopping Mary, and from the look on Bailey's face, he was slowly realizing there was more to her than a little gal who was real good at talking on the phone.

He scrunched his lips together as if there was an unpleasant taste in his mouth. "Now you're being silly, sweetheart, especially because I already have someone in custody for Henry Fielding's murder."

"You do?" This was news. Who would he have arrested?

"Who?" Mary asked.

"Bubba Jenkins. The owner of the boat. We found him hiding out in a room at the back of the bowling alley. I guess he went underground right after we found Henry. He has a list of priors and was out on parole. The guy's as guilty as the day is long. Guys like Bubba are a dime a dozen. They get drunk, and then they get behind the wheel of a boat. Figure I'll get him for both murders."

Mary's tone of voice changed from anger to astonishment. "Did he confess?"

Bailey looked perturbed. "Not that it's any of your business, but no. We'll get the evidence we need and make sure Mr. Jenkins doesn't see the light of day for the rest of his life."

"Wait a minute," Mary said. "You arrested someone just because he was hiding out? I don't think that's a crime in Texas."

"It is when you've murdered someone." He pulled the burning cigarette out of the ashtray, knocked off the ash, and put it to his lips.

Bubba Jenkins didn't have a chance with this guy. Guilty until proven guilty. This was the kind of case he could ram through the courts and base it all on Mr. Jenkin's record. No need to dig too deep. I would not let that happen. "What was his motive? Have you checked his alibi?"

Bailey rose. "Enough. I don't have to explain myself to you or anyone else. Get out of my office and keep on going until you hit the street. Officer Oliva, you can expect a reprimand in your file by tomorrow. You need to learn not to disrespect the higher-ups like you did today. Things might be different from where you are from, but this is America, sweetie."

"Excuse me? I was born right down the road in Camden General Hospital. I am an American."

"Right," he said, taking her by the elbow and walking her to the hall, shutting both of us outside.

We started walking to the lobby, our footsteps now a direct reverse of what they were when we entered, so full of purpose.

"That went well, don't you think?" I asked under my breath.

"Walk in the park," Mary answered.

It was later in the evening when Mary called me. Her voice was low, and looking at the time on the clock, she and John had probably just put the kids to bed, and she was speaking on her living room phone.

"How's it going?" I hated to ask because I already knew the answer. With Detective Bailey in the same office she was in, things couldn't go well.

"I don't know, Dot. When I joined the police force, I was excited about having someone who looked like me working with families that I knew. Maybe in the past, they were misunderstood, bullied, and cheated. I wanted to make things right and help women who were in a dangerous situation with their husbands. I wanted to help other Mexicans who were being treated like second-class citizens. After working with Detective Bailey, I'm thinking it was all a pipe dream. How stupid was I to think I could make things better? Why didn't I figure out that I would have to go up against the same unfair conditions in my job that I was trying to get rid of in the police department's treatment of people like me?"

Mary's voice broke as she told me what was on her mind. She was trying not to cry. Ever since I met Mary, I have admired her. She was the first person to take me seriously on the day I waited to see Detective Sprague with a theory on a local murder. Not only that, but she shared half her sandwich with me because Officer Jerry lied about how long I'd have to wait. She was compassionate, and it didn't matter what color my skin was. Physically, we were the exact opposites; mentally, emotionally, and intellectually, we were the same. Hearing her talk like this made me sad. It was the sound of her hope being lost.

"Mary, I'm so sorry. I would say, is there anything I can do, but I feel like I've already caused enough problems for you?"

"That's sweet, Dot. You think you are unbeatable, but I don't think this will surprise you. Bailey not only dislikes Mexicans, but he dislikes women. You know he's single? How did that one get away?"

"What woman would put up with him?"

"The thing is, I'm tired. Tired of fighting and tired of having to say yes, sir, when I want to say what the hell? My cousin Ina has a beauty shop, and she told me she would teach me how to cut hair. I'm seriously thinking about taking her up on the offer. Since they demoted me to dispatch, I'll probably be making about the same amount of money, so it won't make a difference."

"You can't cut hair. You are a great policewoman."

"Yeah, the best one on the force. Oh, and the only one on the force. It feels like I'm always at a disadvantage. No, I don't have the fight in me anymore. It's not worth it."

"Don't give up like this. Fight that jerk. Ben is going to find out more about him. He hasn't told me anything yet, but if anybody can dig up dirt on somebody, it's Ben. Hold out until we find out if Bailey's been in trouble anywhere else."

"I know you love Ben, but I don't think he's that good at digging up dirt. If Bailey ever did anything bad, then you can bet the boys in blue will protect that idiot to their dying day, and besides, we don't even know if he has done anything. Perhaps he's just having a bad time here in Camden, and he's taking it out on us."

"Okay. But please, as a gift to me, don't give up yet. Give it another week. Will you promise to try?"

Mary paused for a moment and then let out a sigh. "One week. That's it."

"Thank you. If you leave, who will be there to make sure that people don't get misjudged or arrested unfairly because they don't look like the cops?"

After we hung up the phone, Mary's sadness weighed heavily on me. I had a hard time falling asleep that night. I knew, like Mary, I needed to stay the course. I needed to be Henry's voice. Henry enlisted as Chad, which gave Chad a motive for killing him. It didn't seem to be a powerful motive, so the thing I needed to know was what would drive him to kill somebody. As I tossed back and forth, I wrestled with the idea that I was wrong and Bubba Jenkins hit Henry, but then I had to ask myself: what was his motive and what was he doing with the son of the local mortician? These two never cross paths. But then, was Bubba also involved in the random murder of Betty Weaver? That made little sense.

Chapter Seventeen

The next morning, I was bleary-eyed when I went to work and barely made it to lunch. During my lunch break, Ellie asked me to stop by the bridal shop so I could look at a couple of material swatches for my wedding gown. I tried to put her off, but she insisted she needed to order the material so she would have plenty of time to sew the dress. Even though I had picked out a style, all I could think was that we were marching the curse closer and closer to the door. I pulled up to Bluebonnets Dress Shop around noon and found Ellie sitting in her lawn chair while Barbara was out working with a customer.

"You made it. Wait till you see the material I found for you."

There was a clanking coming from the back room, and I raised an eyebrow at Ellie. In the past, I had heard the efficient whirring sounds of the sewing machine, but never anything like this.

"What's going on back there?"

She dismissed the racket with a wave of her hand in the air. "Oh, that's Al. We've been having trouble with the toilet, and he is trying to fix it. Lord help us. The worst idea you can ever have is to ask an electrician to fix your toilet. He's been swearing at that thing for the last hour." Ellie reached for a box and pulled out a brown manila envelope with my name on it. Inside were three swatches, all silk. There was barely any difference between them. "Which one do you like?"

"Is this a trick question?" I held each delicate silk square up to the light.

Ellie looked unsure of herself as she pushed the tiny silk squares closer. "These three fabrics are distinctly different. Look at this one. It has a little more shine, and this one," she picked up the fabric and pulled at the corners. "It has a little more stretch to it. And the third one, well, that's the most expensive of the three, but I think it would really drape well."

Her explanation helped, but they still looked the same to me. "Gee, Ellie, I trust you on this. Any of those three is fine with me. Which one is it easiest for you to sew?"

"Are you sure? They're all easy to sew."

"Yes, I'm sure. You pick out the material for me." I said, hoping she wouldn't ask me again. I had no idea which fabric to choose and didn't want to be forced to lie and say I preferred one over the other. "I will rely on your expertise. "

"Great, then we'll take the one that has a bit of stretch to it. After the last bride needed the gown out in the center, I do like a dress that has a little give. You're not going to need the bride's last-minute expansion alteration, will you?"

It was obvious what she was implying. "No. The dress will fit just fine from the day we fit it to the day I wear it."

Ellie turned her head to the side and gave me a little smile. "Good for you. Staying a virgin until your wedding night."

"Now, I didn't necessarily say that."

"Why Dot? You're pretty good at keeping a secret, even from me."

Al came out from the back holding a wrench, the front of his overalls wet. "Ellie Darlin, I think we're going to have to replace that toilet. I can't seem to fix it."

"Well, before we fork out the cash for an all-new toilet, let me call the plumber. Yes, I know it'll cost more money, but let me get one more opinion before you declare it dead."

"Hi, Al."

"Hi Dot, how are you doing?"

Now that I had Al right in front of me, I wanted to know what he thought about Bubba being arrested for the murder of Henry Fielding. "Did you hear about Bubba?"

"Oh yeah. The Camden Police Department can't seem to get it right on this one. What would Bubba have to do with the Fielding boy? It's crazy."

"Detective Bailey said Bubba had a history. Prior crimes?"

"Yeah, he's got prior crimes. He got into a bar fight last year, so he was out on probation. That boat he uses on the lake was his daddy's, because he certainly couldn't have bought it himself. It's his pride and joy. He kept complaining about it, always being full of someone else's trash when he got to it. Bubba has had problems with alcohol. He likes himself some whiskey, but I've never seen him drive crazy or act crazy. He's one of those drunks who can hold his liquor."

"Did you hear he was hiding out in a back room in the bowling alley?" I asked.

"I did. I feel sorry for the guy because once you've been put in jail, if there's a crime happening anywhere around you, you immediately not only get blamed for it but get convicted for it. So often, that's the way we do it here in Texas. I don't blame him for hiding out one iota."

All the evidence was circumstantial, and I didn't think Bubba did it either. Still, a man with a record is the first one the police will point to.

I turned to Ellie. "What do you think of Chad Doggett as a suspect?"

Ellie had been writing down notes on a pad of paper and was stapling the fabric swatch to the top. At the mention of Chad Doggett's name, she looked up. "Oh, you mean the young man who didn't want to serve his country so badly that he sent Henry Fielding there to take it over for him? Ever since I heard about that from you, I don't think much of that punk," Ellie said.

Barbara, Ellie's new assistant, was waiting on a bride and her mother. "Listen, you have Barbara here working. How would you like to go on a little secret mission with me?"

A sparkle shone in Ellie's eyes. "That sounds very exciting."

Al gave me a wary look. "Don't get my bride and the mother of my child into any trouble. Do you hear me?"

"Yes, sir." I pulled Jeff Hudson's card out of my purse. "Call this number and see if we can get this guy to come to your house to demonstrate a vacuum."

"We don't need a new vacuum," Al said.

"He's right. We don't. Why would I want to subject myself to a sales pitch?"

"Because this is Chad Doggett's best friend."

Ellie raised her head slowly. "Ah, I see. That guy. Is it okay he ran into me at Chad's brother's wedding?"

"Oh, yes. Even better. He won't suspect he's being set up. You're just a mother-to-be looking to provide the cleanest home possible for your new baby."

An hour later, we waited in Ellie's new home for Jeff to show up with his vacuum. I briefed Ellie on my plan. "You play helpless female and ask Jeff for some information on something silly having to do with the vacuum. Make sure you play really dumb so that he gets into lots of explaining. Once he feels comfortable and thinks he has the upper hand in making a sale, start asking him about Chad. Try to get him to tell you about the day Henry was killed. He might give away what Chad was doing. I would do this, but I don't think he trusts me."

Ellie whispered. "Got it. Where will you be?"

"I'll be hiding in the kitchen."

An hour later, I stood in Ellie's kitchen waiting for Jeff. The doorbell rang, and Ellie stood straighter, pulling at the sides of her dress. I could see her through the slats of the shutters that separated the kitchen counter leading into the dining room. From there, I had a clear view of the den as well.

Ellie was lying on her befuddled housewife dialect. "So, you're saying this vacuum is so light, I'll barely know I'm working?"

"Yes, ma'am. It'll be like doing nothing at all. A life of leisure."Jeff started up the vacuum and then invited Ellie to push it. She did and then, with a touch of melodrama, put her hand to her mouth. "My, my. It's as light as a feather."

Jeff shut off the vacuum. "It sure is. Let me ask, is there a reason you're in the market for a new vacuum? I was surprised to get your call. As a matter of fact, it's the first time anyone has ever called me. How did you know where to find me?"

Ellie stumbled a bit. "I was at Chad Doggett's wedding, and someone told me you sold vacuums and after that, I guess it was just kismet because they had your card. I'm expecting a baby, you know."

"Well, congratulations." He nodded and smiled.

"Thank you very much. I'm so excited to bring a baby into this world, even if there have been some dicey things going on in Camden. Did you hear about that boy who got hit by the boat? Henry Fielding was his name, I think? "

"Just terrible. I heard about it the next day. I was out with my best buddy at the movie theaters in Dallas."

"Hard to believe something like this could happen in the town of Camden. What movie did you and your buddy see?"

Jeff opened his mouth like a fish gasping for air. Finally, he said, "*The Sound of Music.*"

That was a strange choice for two young guys, but it was also the movie everyone was talking about. It didn't fit. I could see them watching a more man-centered movie, not a nun and a bunch of kids. He was a terrible liar. Not so smooth without his wise-cracking buddy next to him. I couldn't stand it and came out from behind the kitchen shutters. "That's interesting, Jeff. I never thought of you and Chad as Julie Andrews fans."

Jeff dropped the handle of the vacuum he had been holding, making it clunk across the floor. His face reddened. "What's going on here? Was this all a setup? Dot? What are you? Nancy Drew?" His eyes went from confusion to anger. I could tell he did not like surprises.

"I'm just trying to figure out what really happened to Henry Fielding. I'd like you to meet my cousin Ellie. I wasn't sure if you would talk to me, but you were extremely helpful in letting us know where your buddy Chad was on the day of Henry's death. Now, are you seriously trying to tell me you went to *The Sound of Music?*"

He looked over at Ellie with disgust. "I'll bet you're not even expecting a baby."

Ellie held up both hands in protest. "Why would I ever lie about something like that?"

Jeff walked over and put his face so close to mine I could smell Juicy Fruit gum on his breath. "Listen to me; I'm tired of you nosing around our business. Why would it even matter where we were when that loser died? If you know what's good for you, you're going to leave this alone. If you don't, you will be sorry." He quickly packed up the vacuum and started for the door.

"Was that a threat?" I asked as he slammed his case shut.

He nodded to Ellie. "Thank you for giving me the chance to demonstrate this outstanding product. If you are interested in purchasing a vacuum, you can call me." Just like that, he was back to his job selling vacuums, brushing the dirt of our questions aside.

Once he was gone, Ellie grabbed my hands. "Oh, that was so much fun. Call me in on all your secret missions. You really got him hot under the collar."

I wasn't so sure I wanted to do that, as I recalled Al's last statement. I was to keep his wife and the mother of his child safe. Trying to catch a murderer wasn't what I would call safe.

Chapter Eighteen

That evening, after returning from a workday that included a vacuum cleaner demonstration, I was still a little rattled by my confrontation with Jeff at Ellie's house. I knew he was protective of Chad, but I did not know just how protective he was. Every time I saw Chad, Jeff was always there next to him. The two were quite a pair. Something more than best friends. Their relationship started when they were in school together, and they were doing everything they could to keep it that way. Ben had been working on what he could find out about Detective Bailey and was returning from Dallas, where he thought he might find out more. He called me when he got home and suggested trying out a new restaurant in town called the "Oil Rigger." As I got ready for my date, Arlene, my landlady, called up the stairs to announce a visitor. Eagerly, I donned my coat and hurried downstairs, each step echoing with anticipation. As I reached the bottom, I went into Ben's waiting arms, enveloped in the comfort of his embrace, longing to forget the tensions of the day. His lips met mine in a tender kiss, igniting a sense of relief and belonging.

"Wow. I need to go out of town more often. Did you miss me?" Ben's smile was infectious, erasing the shadows of the day. His deep brown hair had a slight curl, rebelliously attempting to rest upon his forehead. I kissed him again. "I guess you did."

Arlene stood in the doorway of her kitchen. "It's a good thing you two are getting married soon. If you wait much longer, that horse is going to get out of the barn." Ben laughed, and I blushed. I wasn't sure if Arlene realized the double entendre she had made. I laughed, too, eventually.

"Come on, Arlene. It's been two whole days. We're young and in love." Ben turned back to me. "Let's go out for dinner. I'm starving."

Once we got ourselves settled at the restaurant, Ben was running his finger along the menu choices, trying to figure out what to order. Large pictures of oil riggers adorned the walls around the black leather booths, capturing the theme. The full bar featured an interesting display of hard hats hanging on the wall behind it. I decided to try the hamburger. That was a dish that was hard to mess up, so it would be my entry into the world of their menu. Once decided, Ben looked up, smiled, and put his hand on top of mine. His large fingers encased my smaller ones, and then he squeezed gently. His gaze held a curious glint as he leaned in, eager to catch up on the events of the past few days. "I knew you were excited to see me, but now I'm curious to know what's been going on the last couple of days."

I started unrolling my napkin wrapped around the silverware. "Well, it hasn't been good. Did you hear they arrested Bubba Jenkins for the murder of Henry Fielding?"

"Bubba Jenkins. It might have been his boat, but there is no evidence that he was the one who was driving it. It all leads back to him, huh?"

"You've been gone too long, Mr. Dalton. You've forgotten about the modern police methods of the Camden PD or the lack thereof. Detective Bailey assumed that because it was his boat, it must have been him. It didn't help that Bubba has a criminal record."

"Ah," he said, unwrapping his silverware. "According to the old investigative theory, sometimes a zebra is a zebra."

I didn't know what he was talking about, but he continued talking. "Now Bubba Jenkins is sitting in jail, and I think the actual murderer is still out there."

"And that would be?"

"I think it's Chad Doggett. I uncovered some information while you were gone," I confided, a sense of urgency creeping into my voice. "You know Chad Doggett paid Henry to go to the recruiting office in Dallas using his name so he could get a rejection letter? Of course, they wouldn't take anybody with a hearing loss. It was a brilliant plan until Henry ended up dead."

The waiter came over to take our order, and we quickly ordered and sent him on his way.

"Wait, a minute. Chad Doggett paid Henry to get out of going into the service. Wow, I know some guys don't want to go, but that's amazing. Now that makes some sense. At least now we have a motive. Why didn't you call me?"

"The phone lines go both ways. You could have called me."

Ben leaned closer. "You've got me there. I guess I must be getting a little egotistical thinking that you want me to know everything that's going on in your life. You're an independent woman. I'm just not sure how this is all going to work when we have children."

Children hadn't even entered my mind. I was still worried whether Ben would live past the wedding with this god-awful curse that was becoming more real every day. "Children? How many children were you thinking?"

"Maybe 4 or 5? Twins run in my family, you know."

I gulped. Knowing about everything that Ellie was going through now, being pregnant four or five times seemed like an awful lot to ask, even if you loved somebody.

Ben tapped his fingers on the table. "How many do you want?"

"How about one at a time? Let's see how we do with the first one. If we can keep it alive, we might think about a second one."

Ben laughed. "I missed you, Dot." He reached over and kissed me. After our burgers came, Ben said between bites, "Do you have any kind of proof that Chad could have done it?"

"Not really. Hey, I had the stupid idea that I would figure out what Chad's alibi was on the night of Henry's murder. I knew I couldn't ask Chad, so Ellie and I trapped Jeff by asking him to show us a vacuum. He's a vacuum cleaner salesman. I hid out until things got uncomfortable for Ellie. He wasn't too happy when he realized what was going on."

"I'll bet. And what did he say?"

"He said they were at the movies, watching, of all things, *The Sound of Music*. As hard as I try, I don't see those two guys following the adventures of the singing Von Trapp family." A hint of skepticism colored my words.

"Not exactly a young man's movie, especially when most of the women in it are dressed as nuns. Yeah, I'll try to ask him a few more questions, but it might be hard. My mother already has a vacuum."

I thought about the menacing look that Jeff had given me today and wasn't sure if Ben's getting involved might trigger the curse. It might be better to keep Ben away.

"Maybe, but I think if we want to question him again, he's not going to cooperate."

Ben took a bite of his fries. "Maybe so, but it doesn't sound like Bubba Jenkins is guilty, and we cannot let an innocent man go to jail. Which brings me to my next point."

"Yes?"

"I did a little background digging on Detective T.J. Bailey. He has quite a checkered past."

As luck would have it, as he talked about Detective Bailey, the detective himself walked into the restaurant. The waiter showed him to a table, but before he sat down, he scanned the room, his eyes lighting on us. Upon seeing us, his face formed into a scowl. I was about as happy to see him as he was to see us. I whispered to Ben. "Lower your voice. He just walked in."

"Speak of the devil," Ben muttered under his breath, his tone tinged with irony. "I'll be quick about it. It seems Detective Bailey got into trouble at his last police station. He got into a disagreement with another officer, and it turned into a fistfight."

"I can believe that. Someone who bullies another officer like he's bullying Mary is not too far from committing violence."

"So true, but here's the kicker. The other officer? He was black. Bailey had been written up several times for harassing this officer, but he repeatedly told his superiors that he did not believe that a black man should be on the police force. I guess he thinks Black people are for arresting and not doing the arresting."

"What a jerk. How did he end up in Camden?"

"And that is the $64,000 question. Surely, he had to have references to come here."

"If he gave them an actual reference."

"What do you mean?"

"What if all he needed was a typed letter using his last station's letterhead and a number to call? Whoever the chief of police talked to could have been anybody. When Sprague quit suddenly in the middle of a major murder case, the chief had to be desperate."

"I see what you mean. The other police department could have also given him a reference just to get rid of him."

The waiter put our bill on the table, and Ben picked it up and fished his wallet out of his pocket. I watched Detective Bailey as he ordered his food, being particular about how they cooked his steak. The waiter he was speaking to had warm brown skin. I would not want to be the waiter who brought a well-done steak if he ordered medium-rare. As the waiter took the menu away, Bailey looked at our table and winked and waved.

Chapter Nineteen

The next day, I was knee-deep in sorting a fresh batch of prayer cards from the printer, each one a little reminder of life's fragility. That's when Peter sneaked up on me, mum in hand, for one of the visitation rooms. He peered over my shoulder with a concerned look on his face.

"Oh boy, we've got a mistake here," he said, pointing to the card.

"A mistake? Where?" I asked, feeling a little perturbed at finding a mistake. I meticulously proofread all the information before sending it to Mr. Doyle's Print Shop on Fourth Street. If there was a mistake on these cards, we were in for a world of trouble, especially since there wasn't time to fix it before the funeral. Oliver would blow a gasket, and he already had enough on his plate.

"It's Johnston, not Johnson," Peter clarified, shaking his head.

I squinted at the card. "Seriously? I must've missed that." Fixing this mess would be a headache. I was generally good with minor details, but with everything going on in my life, I had missed this one.

"Well, at least we caught it before the family did," Peter said with a quick smile. It didn't bother him. Why would it? He wasn't the one who was going to have to redo everything. "I'll give Oliver a heads up."

"Thanks, Peter. I owe you one," I said, trying to look grateful.

"He's a pretty nice guy. I wouldn't worry about it. I don't think this is a fireable offense."

"I hope not. I kind of have a little reputation."

Peter looked uncomfortable.

"No," I blurted. "Not that kind of reputation. It's just that I don't seem to stay employed for very long."

Then he looked puzzled. "You? I think you're great. If I had to guess, the problem was with your boss, not you."

If he only knew.

As Peter wandered off to deal with the mum, he turned back with a mischievous grin. "Now that you mention it, I did hear some interesting gossip about you at The Uphill the other night."

My stomach dropped at the mention of The Uphill Bar—where the more the drinks flowed, the more the people told the secrets of the town. "Oh? Do I even want to know?" I replied, bracing myself for the worst.

"They're calling you The Curse of Camden," Peter said, trying to stifle a laugh. "But don't worry, it's more out of fascination than fear."

I let out a nervous chuckle. "Great, just what I needed," I muttered, feeling like I was living in a bad soap opera.

Peter made a flapping motion with his hand. "Ah, it's all good fun. No harm done. I wouldn't sweat it, Dot. Folks over at The Uphill are more dazzled by your mysterious aura than spooked by it," Peter reassured me, his voice carrying a hint of amusement. "As for curses, well, let's just say I'm in the business of dealing with the departed, and I haven't seen any ghosts yet. As for the afterlife, well, I'll believe it when I see it."

That was surprising to hear. No one around me ever said they didn't believe in life after death. It was also daring for a funeral employee. Peter reached to pick up the mum again. "I'll tell you what. I won't care about your so-called curse, and you can keep it quiet you're working with a heathen. That work?"

I laughed as the phone rang. "Works for me."

When I picked up the phone, Ellie's voice was hushed. "You'll never guess who just sauntered into Bluebonnets."

"Let me guess—Jeff with a brand-new deluxe vacuum cleaner," I quipped, a smile playing on my lips. Ellie rarely called me during work hours unless it was of the utmost importance.

"Close, but not quite. It was Mrs. Doggett," Ellie revealed, her voice a conspiratorial whisper. "She dropped by to repay us the money we gave her for the dress. She wants to do it in installments. Isn't that a peach?"

It was sweet and not unexpected because Mrs. Doggett had always been so kind to everyone she knew. Owing money for a dress would bother her. "Has she accepted that it was her own son who took the money out of her stash?"

"Of course not. That boy can do no wrong in her eyes. But here is what she said that's interesting. Chad's leaving town."

"He is?"

"Yup. He's heading to Dallas to get a job."

"What brought all this on?"

"Now that everybody knows he faked his enlistment rejection, Big Buck couldn't take it. He threw Chad out. Mrs. Doggett said he spent the night at his buddy Jeff's house. He had to sneak back in when his dad went to work so he could pack."

"Poor Mrs. Doggett. This must be tearing her apart." I had never heard her say anything negative about her son. The thing that got under my skin was that Chad never appreciated her praise. After a while, if a person keeps hearing how wonderful he is, he believes it, even if he's not so terrific. Chad's leaving town might be a good thing for him, but it was terrible for my investigation. Was he leaving because his father threw him out or was he leaving to escape justice? In Dallas, it would be a lot harder for the Camden Police to chase him down and question him, but the way they were going with Bubba Jenkins, they might not even try.

"I can't believe Chad and Jeff are going their separate ways," I said.

"They're not. Jeff is quitting his job at Hoover. He has a little money, so he's going to pay the first month's rent. Chad has very little money of his own."

"As much as Chad drinks, he will not do well. If I had to guess, any money he's made here in Camden went to alcohol. He'd better look for employment at the bars first."

Ellie laughed, and I heard the tinkle of the bells on the door of Bluebonnets. "You may be on to something there. I have to go, but I knew you would want to know."

After we hung up the phone, I thought about Chad's adventure. There was something different about this behavior I had never seen before in Chad. He was leaving Camden and the security of his doting mother. But he had Jeff to hold him up. I wasn't sure if this would work. How was it going to be when Jeff found out that Chad was planning to drink his way through this new life they were creating? When I first met Chad and Jeff, they had the world by the tail. Now, it seemed the opposite.

I didn't realize Oliver was standing by my desk. He clenched his hands in the front, looking nervous. "Dot. I was wondering if I could ask you if you'd heard anything more about Henry trying to enlist. Peter was just telling me a rumor going around town."

Great. Peter told him about the rumors of a curse going around. "Yes?"

"Do you think Henry went and enlisted for someone else and was rejected because of his hearing loss?"

I hated to have to do it, but it was time to tell Oliver my theory.

Chapter Twenty

The following day, rain was pouring down relentlessly. In Texas, a spring storm is a unique experience—the sound of raindrops hitting the roof, the fresh scent of wet earth filling the air. One minute, it's warm and lovely, but then the sky unleashes a torrential downpour, flooding yards and transforming puddles into car-sized pools. I was on the blacklist at the police station, so I called up Mary to see if she wanted to brave the weather and meet at the funeral home, or we could grab a bite somewhere.

"I'd love to, but I can't. We're saving every penny we can in case I get fired, for God knows what."

"Fair enough. Wanna swing by here? I've got a sandwich stashed away," I suggested.

There was a pause on the other side. "I'd rather not, but I guess it is what it is. Sure, I'll come over to Death Valley."

I couldn't help but chuckle. "Don't say that when you're here. Neva would have a fit."

"What? You think it won't catch on?" Mary quipped back.

I thought about Oliver and his mom, Neva. I had never heard any gallows humor from them, at least not around me.

As I listened to my stomach grumble while looking through an invoice for a set of headstones, Dina White rushed in the door, collapsing her umbrella. Her cap, made of transparent plastic, was embellished with subtle flower patterns and fastened with a chin strap. I'd seen these rain bonnets for sale in the drugstore, and when she took it off, her carefully sprayed hair looked perfect. I would need to remember to grab one the next time I was out. My hair usually curled a little in the rain, so it would be nice to tame it.

"Is Oliver in?" Dina folded the bonnet and stuck it in her raincoat pocket.

"He is. I think he's downstairs. Let me see if I can find him." I pushed the button on my phone and spoke over the intercom in the embalming area. "Oliver?"

"Thanks. I'm here on my lunch break, so I can't stay long." Dina glanced at her watch.

The intercom buzzed. "Yes, Dot. What can I do for you?"

"Dina White is here to see you."

There was a pause, then, "Oh. Okay. I'll be up in a few minutes." Oliver sounded surprised and then a little nervous. After seeing them together at the funeral, it was clear something had started up between them.

She took off her yellow rain slicker. "I hope I'm not interrupting anything. I know Oliver's very busy now that the funeral home has reopened."

"You probably are, but I wouldn't worry about it. Oliver's thrown himself into work since Henry's passing. A friendly face might be just what he needs," I reassured her.

Dina's pleasant smile lit up her face. She shared many similarities with Oliver. There was a certain elegance that emanated from her. I'd bet you'd never see her yelling rudely at the umpire at a ball game or cutting in front of somebody at the bank. No. I knew that Oliver was interested in her. She possessed a genuine kindness that was hard to resist.

Neva came from her office in the back, holding the Johnson/Johnston reorder. "Dot. Are you the one who made this mistake?" Her eyes had been on the paper she was holding, but when she looked up, she noted Dina.

"Good morning, Mrs. White. What can we do for you today?" She was all business. Neva was the mama bear of Fielding Funeral Home, and I had to wonder if a romantic involvement with her only son would be a threat to her. She wasn't very welcoming to Henry's mother at the funeral. When she wasn't giving her scornful stares, she was avoiding her.

"Oh, I'm here to see Oliver," Dina said quickly.

"About what?" Neva asked.

Dina tried to answer, but Oliver came in and saved her. "Dina? What a pleasant surprise." The smile on Oliver's face was genuine. "What brings you here today in this terrible weather?"

Dina glanced out the window and then back at Oliver. "I wanted to ask you something."

Oliver nodded pleasantly. "Sure. Go ahead."

Neva made no movement to go, but I picked up the watering can to give them some privacy.

"No need for that," Neva said. "I already watered."

I put the can back down and went back to my desk, feeling bad I was about to eavesdrop.

Dina took a breath and forged ahead. "It's just that I have this wedding to go to. My cousin Deb is getting married and well," she trailed off, her voice unsure. I felt an excitement rise in me as I figured out she was about to ask Oliver to go with her. I couldn't be happier for him. He deserved this. Better yet, he needed it.

She stumbled on with her words. "Well, would you consider helping me out and going with me? The boys will be with my parents that night."

I waited for Oliver to say yes, but he began stuttering. "D-Dina. That's so nice of you to think of me, but...well..."

Neva cut Oliver off before he could finish. "We're very busy here at the funeral home. The average person has no idea what we do here."

Dina took a quick breath and grabbed for her rain slicker. "You're right. I know you're busy here. I was being silly." She pulled her arms through her coat.

"No. It's not that. It's that I'm still a mess after what happened to Henry. I'd feel—this is going to sound strange," he put his hand on his chin as he thought. "I'd feel guilty having fun with Henry dead."

"Of course, you would," Neva said, sounding eager to back him up and drive her right out the door. "We are still in a period of mourning as a family."

Dina put her rain bonnet back on her head, trying to make a quick exit. "Sorry to have bothered you," she muttered as she made her way out the door.

Oliver watched her, a longing in his eyes.

Neva turned to me, holding up the invoice. "This was a costly mistake.

Please double-check the spelling from now on." With that, she marched back to her office, two problems solved.

"Oliver?" I asked, not sure how he would feel about what I was going to say. I considered him a friend, but he was also my boss. "You should have gone with her."

"No. I'm not ready." He turned to walk back to the basement. "I don't deserve it. I let my son get killed." He escaped to the stairwell.

Not going to the wedding with Dina was the saddest thing I'd ever heard. It wasn't his fault someone killed Henry, but somehow, he had misplaced the blame. Now, he would punish himself, even though he found a lovely woman who might help him get through his overwhelming loss. Worse, his mother was discouraging romance for her own reasons, causing him to double down on not allowing anything good in his life. Like the rain clouds outside, I felt a few had slipped inside, hanging over us, graying out the colors of our lives.

An hour later, Mary and I sat huddled in the front lobby between the nasturtiums and carnations. I quickly told Mary what I'd found out about T.J. Bailey from Ben. "So, Mary, there you have it. He has already lost a job because of the way he treats other people. All you have to do is tell your superiors that, and you'll get him out of there and out of your hair."

Mary shrugged and watched the rain marching down the front window. "If it were only that easy. One party can't complain about another party unless there is a sense of equality between them. In my case, I'm not looked at as an equal over there. That's why I got demoted to dispatcher. Do you think Jerry enjoyed having me right there in the same office as him? Jerry has worked at the front desk of the police department for ten years, and suddenly, he has a partner. But I'm not a guy he can go down to the bar and have a beer with after work, no. Do they want a person of Mexican heritage with two children? Not likely. I don't fit the poster. They want that strapping young white guy with a crew cut and the ability to follow every order, no matter how stupid it might be. I'm the exact opposite of that, so if I were to go forward with a complaint, do you think anyone would listen to me?"

"When you put it that way, I'm surprised you've stayed as long as you have. It sounds incredibly bleak."

"Dot, I appreciate what you're doing here, and I know you are not like them. You see me for me, and that's all. I value that from you, and I hope that in the future, there will be more people like you out there."

I knew I wasn't the only one who felt like I did. "You know, Mary. People look at me and see a dumb blond. They size me up as a mixture of Gidget and Marilyn Monroe, and no matter what I say, they keep that impression of me. You don't seem to care what I look like, and I value that from you as well. Listen, if you don't say something, he's going to continue to get away with this. He'll hurt somebody else because he doesn't approve of them."

Mary's lips were pressed tightly together as she focused intently on the rain streaking down the window. I had finally struck a nerve. We had to get rid of Bailey. "Think of your kids. They need to see that you're willing to fight against people like Bailey."

"You don't understand. It's easy to be a blond in this world," she grunted. For the first time, I heard anger coming out of her voice. I was making her angry by talking about this and telling her things she didn't want to hear. She was David, and Bailey was Goliath.

"What can I do?"

"Try staying out of it. Can you do that much? Sometimes, you just don't know when to quit. You cannot save the world all by yourself, and I didn't ask you to save me."

"I'm not trying to save you. I'm just trying to do what's right."

"Then maybe doing what's right is leaving this. Let me handle it in my way. You underestimate Bailey. He's quickly made a lot of friends here, and well, he's bigger than I am. I don't like being in a room alone with him."

This was the first time Mary had ever said anything like this, and it made me wonder what had happened between them. Had Bailey done something untoward to Mary? "What are you trying to say? Just how afraid of Bailey are you?"

"If I tell you this, promise that you will not tell John, because once he finds out, I will never get to be a cop anywhere ever again. I know I said I'm thinking about quitting, but I want that to be my decision and not his. Please promise me that."

132

"I promise."

Mary gazed at her fingers and then started moving one hand across the other, palm and back. I waited for her to tell me what seemed so uncomfortable to say. "We were alone back in the file room. He put his hand on my shoulder." Her voice fell away.

"What? What did he do?"

"It was nothing. He squeezed my shoulder. Hard."

"Do you think he was making a pass at you?"

"No. I think he was making it very clear that he's bigger and stronger than I am."

"Oh, my gosh. Mary, if you were a man, he never would have pulled anything like that. We need to report what he did."

"Right. Report it. Get this into that head of yours. I can report it all I want, but nobody is going to believe me. It's just the way things are."

"Well, that's not fair. How come you have a different set of rules? You have to do something."

"Okay, but it has to be something that will give me the least amount of blowback from the chief and the other cops."

"I'm sorry that I don't always understand what's going on with you. If you can forgive me, I will try to do better. Sometimes, I make these assumptions that everybody's life is just like mine, and it isn't. Although I have had a boss chase me around a desk, I can understand that. I didn't like it, and now you're having to put up with it."

Mary shrugged. "I forgot about that. We just have to stay strong and make sure that we tell someone, even if it's just each other."

"Yeah, and maybe we'll get the Camden meter maid to keep putting chalk marks on his tire. He should at least get a ticket for that." Nancy Turner was the infamous meter maid of Camden, Texas. Parked cars have a time limit of four hours, and you'd better bet she'd catch a tardy parker one minute later. She wrote tickets faster than a typewriter, and she never missed a day of work. Being a fellow woman who had to work at Camden PD, she'd be glad to do a little harassing of Camden's newest good old boy.

The sound of Mary's laughter echoed in my ears as she left the funeral home that day. She was one of the strongest women I knew, and T.J. Bailey didn't know it yet, but he had met his match.

Chapter Twenty-One

By the next week, things went back to normal at the Fielding Funeral Home, with Oliver teaching Peter, the new assistant, and the flow of business resuming. I was busy with florists calling, coordinating with the Camden Meadows Internment staff, and all of Neva's demands. Working for Oliver was easy, but it could be depressing, and I did what I could to not let it get to me. On Monday, I was wearing a vibrant top adorned with enormous pink and yellow circles paired with a matching pink skirt. Neva, Oliver's mother, approached me, deep in thought, with her hand resting on her chin.

"Dot, that certainly is a very colorful outfit you have on today."

I smoothed out the skirt. "Thank you. I love pink."

"I can tell. I would ask on the days we have people visiting their loved ones that you stick to more somber tones."

"You want me to wear black?" The thought of going to work every day in black made me feel like an extra in a Bela Lugosi movie. They never mentioned funeral wear in the classes at secretarial school. I had dresses in yellow, pink, green, and combinations of other bright colors. When I stood next to Oliver in front of a crowd of mourners all in dark hues, I stuck out like a peacock. I read the fashion magazines, and women weren't adorning themselves in black. I was much more of a peacock than a crow. So, pulling out a black or blue skirt every day had me wanting to change the minute I got home. The outfits in the magazines I looked at when I was at the beauty salon were getting more colorful with every issue, and skirts kept getting shorter. Add a pair of boots, preferably white, and the look is com'lete. Just not for someone's grandma's funeral.

"How about the days when we have nothing going on?" I asked.

"Wear what you like," she answered, but then stopped. "With a business look to it."

Blonds don't pull off black well. That was why Marilyn Monroe stopped them all dead with that white dress over the subway vent. I pulled at the cuff of my blouse and buckled down, going back to typing the obituaries I had to send over to *The Camden Courier*. This was what I spent two years in secretarial school for, but I always imagined something a little more exciting and not so darn quiet.

"Dot?"

I jumped at the sound of Oliver's voice. How long had he been standing behind me? Were all funeral directors like this, or was he just particularly sneaky? "Oliver. You snuck up on me. I didn't hear you."

"That was obvious. Busy doing your job. You know, we had Mrs. Davidson here for almost ten years, and when she told me she was retiring to go live in Arkansas with her sister, I worried I would never find a replacement as efficient as she was. You were the first person I interviewed, and I hired you on the spot. Glad I did. I'm just sorry you've had to go through all this with us. Businesses change and evolve over the years. I never expected the funeral home to change like this, though. It feels different without Henry here."

"If it's any comfort to you, every business I've worked for has gone through some sort of upheaval while I was there." I conveniently left out the part where I was also called The Curse of Camden.

Oliver put his hands in the pockets of the pants of his black suit. "You know, I had a bad feeling when Henry started keeping secrets. I knew something was wrong. Then, at Betty Weaver's funeral, he acted like he was friends with two people who were not his friends. I was curious why it was happening, but I hoped, naively, that Henry had made more friends than Nelson." He gazed out the window at the empty parking lot. "You always hope that for your child. Happiness. I hoped Henry had somehow risen above the past and was starting his life as a young man. It was strange, the changes, but maybe it was time, I thought."

This was the first time Oliver had brought up Chad and Jeff. "Did you know how they treated him in high school?"

"Of course I did. Henry would come home and slam his door. He wouldn't let me in, but I knew he was crying. Now I know that some of those times had to do with those two young men. What kind of kid bullies someone else to enlist in the Army for them? What kind of person is that? They were using him, and my son let them."

"I don't think he did, but that still doesn't connect the fake enlistment to how he died."

"I know, but it gives Chad a reason to kill him. My guess is that he asked him to come along on the boat and intentionally grounded it at a high speed, throwing Henry into the bank."

This was the first time Oliver had said the name of anyone in relation to the death of his son. "You don't think it was Bubba Jenkins?"

"Like I said, I know Bubba. He wouldn't do that. He's a mess, but he's not a killer."

It felt like we knew the facts and could prove them, but the only thing stopping us was that the police weren't choosing to listen.

The next morning, I was typing up notes from a session with a grieving family when Ben came in holding the latest edition of *The Camden Courier*.

"Have you read the paper this morning?" He asked.

"No, sorry. Did you have an article I need to read?" Ben wrote for the paper daily, covering everything from city council meetings to fender benders to murder. I didn't read everything he wrote, but I tried to catch his crime reporting. Some of those articles were about me.

"Good." He mumbled into his collar.

That was a strange response. I'd never seen Ben so happy that I missed his latest article. "Why is that good?" He threw himself into one of the deeply tufted red velvet chairs near my desk.

"Because I need to prepare you. It isn't something you're going to like. Someone wrote a letter to the editor about The Curse of Camden and used your name."

I pushed back from the typewriter. "Who? Who wrote that about me? Can they even do that?"

"It's all pretty weird how it happened. The letter was left at our office and was signed anonymously, so we don't know who wrote it."

"But your editor published it, anyway? Isn't that against the rules at the paper?"

Ben nodded patiently. "It is, but my boss thought this would be an interesting way to show the public some of the crazy things that get written to the editor. He states right at the beginning that what the writer is saying is wrong." He handed me the paper. "Here. Do you want to read it for yourself?"

I closed the steno book I had been using to type up my notes and snatched the paper out of his hand. I turned to the editorial page, and there at the top was the headline: THE CAMDEN CURSE RIDES AGAIN.

"Oh my God," I muttered, feeling a cold sensation flow over me. I read on.

"Dear Reader: We are including this letter today just to show you how outrageous some of the letters are that we receive at the *Courier*. There is no Camden Curse, and we feel it is only right to point this out in defense of the young lady mentioned here, Dot Morgan."

That seemed like a pleasant introduction, but the lettering on the part written by the editor was in italics, whereas the actual letter was in print, which was universal for all the articles in the paper. Did people read italics or skip to what looked like the article? I read further down.

"Dear Editor,

This town is plagued with a curse, and it's amazing that the fine people living here have let it go on for as long as they have. What is the curse, you say? The curse is in the form of a person, Dot Morgan, who has had murders occur in the last three jobs she's been employed at. Don't you think that's a little strange? She is known as The Curse of Camden, and her latest murder victim is Henry Fielding, the poor, deaf son of the town's beloved mortician.

CHAPTER TWENTY-ONE

The sadness of this passing is a blow to us all.

What do we do about this now-yearly occurrence? We need to invite The Curse of Camden, Dot Morgan, to leave our fair city and never look back. I call you to arms. If you see Miss Morgan, tell her to leave...or else."

I put a hand on my heart. "I can't believe you published this. It's amazing somebody actually wrote that about me."

I stared at the newsprint, which was now beginning to blur as my emotions intensified. "What am I going to do? People are going to want me to leave now."

"But the editor said right from the beginning that it was an example of the crazy letters they get. No one is going to say anything."

Ben was delusional.

"Ever hear about the War of the Worlds broadcast? Orson Welles told the world it was a fake, but most people didn't hear that part. They believed everything they heard. How can anyone guarantee that the town will take time to read the editor's notes in italics?

"Dot?" Oliver stood at the door of the basement, his embalming apron still on, the scent of formaldehyde surrounding him. "What's wrong? I could hear your voice from downstairs."

"Everything is wrong. The paper just told the world I'm cursed. A plague on the town. They printed a letter to the editor that told readers to tell me to leave Camden because they say I cause murders to happen."

"That's the silliest thing I've ever heard." Oliver walked over and took the paper from me. He began to read and then put the paper down, turning to Ben.

"Why would they publish something like this?"

"I didn't do it personally, sir, but I wanted Dot to be prepared."

Oliver sat down next to me and said, "Don't worry. We'll protect you, Dot. After all we've been through, you're like my daughter. I'm not going to let anything happen to you."

I felt like he wanted to add one more thing. He wouldn't let anything happen, like what happened to Henry.

When I got to my apartment that night, Arlene had my mail stacked on the table in the hall. On top of the letters was a single envelope with no address, just my name on it. I ripped it open. Written in block letters was this chilling message:

MIND YOUR OWN BUSINESS, OR THINGS WILL GET WORSE.

"Wow, Dot. You sure know how to get the town's attention. I read that letter in the paper and about dropped my cornflakes." Ellie said when I visited her dress shop the next day. "Somebody sure has it out for you."

"Yes, and I have a pretty good idea who that is. I started asking questions about Chad Doggett, and next thing I know, someone is renting billboards and calling me The Curse of Camden."

"He rented a billboard. Which side of town?"

"It's a figure of speech," I said. "Luckily, Oliver said it doesn't matter to him."

"Yeah, well, he has to be wondering if his son would be dead if this Curse of Camden hadn't come to work for him."

I had felt that, too, but I had never voiced it. Did Oliver regret hiring me? Worse, was there some merit to this whole curse thing? What about my family? Were they in danger? Ellie was reaching up to replace a spool of ribbon, and for the first time, I could see a soft rounding in her middle. She was beginning to show.

Ellie gave me a guilty smile. "I'm probably not supposed to be doing that, but Barbara won't be here until eleven, and looking at that roll of ribbon out on the counter would have made me crazy. Anyway, I wanted to raise the idea of another person who might have written that letter."

"Who?"

"From the sounds of all you've told me, Detective Bailey isn't too happy with you, either. Could he have penned the letter?"

I thought of the note that had been slipped into my mail. Hadn't he told me to mind my own business? Was this a way of getting back at me? "I'm not sure what he's capable of if he wants to get me out of his hair. Poor Mary. I don't know how she can stand to work there."

"Poor Mary," she echoed as she leaned on her elbows and looked out onto the main street of Camden. Down and to the right was the hardware store, where Chad and Jeff both had their heads under the hood of an old Chevy. Chad ran to the driver's seat and was attempting to start the car.

"Hmmm. Would you look at that? My most likely suspect seems to be having car trouble. Should I offer my help, or better yet, let the curse do its magic?"

Ellie rolled her eyes. "I don't know Dot. Maybe you should lay off interfering in their lives. I'm sure they won't welcome whatever it is you have to say."

I barely heard Ellie's last words because I was out the door before she could finish saying them. I crossed the street and walked up, unnoticed by either of them.

"Try it again," Jeff said, swirling a finger in the air.

Chad turned the key, making the motor emit a clicking sound.

"It looks like you fellows have a dead battery."

Jeff looked over and then stood up quickly, bumping his head on the hood of the car. "What are you doing here?"

"Oh, I was across the street and saw your car stalled and thought I'd come by to cheer you on."

Chad came out of the driver's seat. "So, you did it." He swept the air with his hand. "You can leave now."

I would not let them off this easily. "Not until I find out where you two are headed on this fine day."

"Not that it's any of your business," Chad said. "But we are driving to Dallas to find work."

I took a breath. "Oh yes, your mother told me you were moving. I thought you'd be gone by now. I know you wish you were gone. Is it a case of expanding your horizons or beating it out of town before they figure out you had a motive to kill Henry? I'm not really sure. One thing I am sure of is that Henry Fielding would be alive today if he hadn't enlisted in the Army for someone else." I planted my feet and crossed my arms.

Jeff spoke as he lowered the hood of the car. "Listen, I know you think you have to prove something, and maybe I was a little harsh with you the other day, but we don't have the time to pick this apart. I had to give two weeks' notice at my job, so we're using today to find an apartment and interview there. Most guys would have walked out on a job like demonstrating vacuums, but I'm trying to do right by them. I had to do it to prove to my mom I was nothing like my old man. What a guy has to do is keep up appearances around here." He blew out a disgusted breath.

"That's good of you, but then I always knew that out of the pair, you were the more responsible one."

Jeff gave a tight-lipped smile. "Anything else?"

"Nope, I just wanted to say you'd better get down to the garage and get a new battery because without it, you're not going anywhere."

Chad slipped a little silver flask into the pocket of his shirt. "Yeah, thanks. We never would have figured that out, Sherlock."

Chapter Twenty-Two

Before I checked into work, I had to make a second stop at the Camden Police Station. If Chad and Jeff were leaving town, it would be harder for the police to track Chad down when they finally realized Bubba Jenkins was the wrong guy. Seeing as Detective Bailey banned me from the station, I would have to come up with a more inventive way of getting in there than walking in front of Officer Jerry. There was a back door the patrolmen used that was next to the employee parking lot. I parked my car a block away and then walked to the parking lot that held one black and white and several personal cars of the officers. No one was there, and when I tried the doorknob, it gave easily. I peeked inside, and no one was in the hall. I tiptoed in, feeling happy with a sense of stealth, but froze when I heard Detective Bailey's voice echoing down the hall. He was laughing with another officer, who was telling a story about how they caught Mr. Wycoff, the pig stealer of the famous Makin' Bacon Caper Ben had been reporting on last week.

"He was pretty dammed surprised. I can sure tell you that. He actually asked me if the other guy had hoof prints to identify Fertile Myrtle."

"What an idiot. I think I'm going to like life in the sticks," Bailey said with a barrel-chested laugh.

As I stepped closer, I could see him through the glass on one side of his office. He had his cowboy boots up on the desk and was smoking a cigar, which was drifting out into the hallway in gray mists. I hit the floor and crawled under the window when Bailey's phone rang. As he answered it, I crawled past the glass, and then once past his line of sight, I stood up and

143

looked around. No one was in the hall, and Mr. Super Detective didn't see me. So much for his abilities of observation.

I darted into the dispatcher's office, where Mary was advising an officer over the radio to make another loop by the bowling alley.

"Mary," I whispered.

She took her headset off and smiled. "What are you doing here? How did you get in here? Did Jerry finally give in to taking a nap at the front desk?"

"It wasn't easy, and I don't have a lot of time. I wanted to let you know Chad Doggett is planning on leaving town. He and his friend Jeff are interviewing for jobs in Dallas, and they could be gone in two weeks. "It will be much harder to track him down in the city."

"That's not good. I hear Dallas has more than a million people there now. I suppose we could check with his mother if we get more evidence against him."

"Okay. I'm not sure she's going to want to cooperate with you, though. She's disillusioned about her little angel, but I still think she's going to protect him, no matter what the cost."

"Even if it's murder?" Mary asked.

"And here you are, the little girl who wanted to be a detective and her sidekick, a humble dispatcher." Detective Bailey filled the door, the cigar still in his mouth. "I thought I told you to stay out of this station. Do you have a problem understanding English, just like your little Mexican girlfriend here?"

I would not let him intimidate me, but my hands shook as I tried to tell him why I was back at the police station. "I wanted to let Mary know something about one of the suspects in the Henry Fielding case."

"A suspect? We don't have any suspects. We have a killer. One, or should I say Uno, for you slow English learners?"

The low rumble of a voice spoke from behind Bailey. "But maybe, hombre, there are more. Dos or even tres?" A tall man stood in the hallway behind Bailey. He wore a badge, but there was something markedly different about him. He was not white. His skin was the same color as Mary's. Next to him was the chief of police, a man I had only seen a few times before. The chief usually kept a low profile, which made me wonder what he actually did. Chief Arthur O'Hara spent more time campaigning than anything else. He promised the voters less crime and a smooth-running, efficient police department. I wasn't sure how he would feel about The Camden Curse standing in front of him, wrecking his crime stats.

The chief moved forward and waved off the smoke that had floated in the hallway. "Put that thing out. It stinks to high heaven."

"Yes, sir." Bailey stepped into the dispatcher's office and put the cigar out in an ashtray.

"Thank you," the chief said. "Detective Bailey, I wanted to introduce you to your new partner. This is Detective Fabio Barrerra. We were lucky enough to get him from the valley."

"Buenos Dias, Detective." Detective Barrerra extended a light brown hand, but Bailey did not respond.

"Partner?" Bailey looked flummoxed. I wished I had my Instamatic camera so I could capture this moment. "Sir, I work primarily alone. I hardly see why you would hire another detective. I barely have enough work to do now. It's a waste of taxpayer money. I think Detective Barrera, " Bailey made a point of overstressing the detective's last name, as if to point out he didn't approve of a Spanish surname, "can pack up his tacos and go work somewhere else."

"Madre Di Dios," Mary said under her breath, slapping a palm to her forehead.

The chief's face clouded over, and his bottom lip tightened up under his mustache. "I beg your pardon. What did you just say?"

Bailey crossed his arms and extended his chest. "With all due respect, we don't need two detectives."

Mary stepped forward. "Don't you mean you refuse to work with Detective Barrera because he's Mexican?"

Bailey's neck snapped as he turned quickly in Mary's direction. "I said nothing of the sort. How dare you put words in my mouth? You are hardly in a position to comment on this situation."

"Yeah," I piped in. "You made sure of that."

The chief smiled. "Then it's settled. I would hate to find out I hired a bigoted detective because if I did, I would have to fire him. Now, why don't you show Detective Barrera where he can put his belongings?"

"Where is his office?" Bailey asked.

"With you, of course. We'll be moving another desk in there this afternoon. In the meantime, you'll have to share. That won't be a problem, will it?"

"No, sir," Bailey mumbled.

Detective Barrera nodded. "Yes, and once I get settled, I would like to hear more about the Henry Fielding case. And Officer," he paused as he addressed Mary.

"Oliva," Mary said.

"Well, Officer Oliva, I don't know why you're doing dispatch, and I will see what I can do to get you back to your proper job, but first, I must know what information you have collected on this case. I admire your persistence in your investigation, even though you were given other duties. That shows you have *corazon para la victima,* a heart for the victim. I always say that overlooking clues can lead to the arrest of the wrong person."

"Yes, sir," Mary said with a smile I hadn't seen in weeks.

"Come on then," Bailey said. "I know you Mexicans move at a slower pace."

Had Bailey not noticed the chief was standing there still? "Bailey. Did you just insult our newest officer because of his nationality?"

"I'm just saying..." Bailey said, looking confident that his chief would back him up.

"I hear what you are saying. I can't believe I hired someone in this day and age who refuses to work with someone with a different skin color. Detective Barrera is as qualified as you are, except for one thing."

Bailey nodded quickly. "And what is that?"

"He's a much nicer person. I've changed my mind. You don't have to show Detective Barrera anything. We need to have a chat in my office."

"But..." Bailey looked at Barrerra and then at the chief.

"Now," the chief said, using a tone of voice I wouldn't want to cross.

As Bailey and the chief went down the hall, Barrera came closer and spoke in a low voice. "I didn't think that would happen so quickly. I was supposed to watch Bailey and report any inappropriate behavior. I didn't expect it to come out in the first minutes of meeting him."

"So, the chief hired you to spy on Bailey?" I asked. "Does that mean you're leaving?"

"No. I just moved here with my wife and kids from the Rio Grande Valley." He turned to Mary. "I have no idea how you've stood the man."

"It's been bad, and I didn't think I'd see this happen today. *Muchas Gracias.*" Mary said.

"Yes, well, now I need to know everything I can about this case. There is a man in jail for this murder, and we both know about people misjudging a suspect without proper evidence."

Mary turned back to the other dispatcher, who was filing her nails. "Dispatch is all yours. I'm going back to police work."

When I told Ben about meeting Detective Barrera later in the day, he couldn't have been more excited. "This is great. I can't believe the chief called somebody in to watch Bailey. Frankly, everyone at *The Camden Courier* wasn't even sure if the chief was working full days over there."

"You should have seen Bailey's face when he got reprimanded for expressing his views on Mexicans."

"Wish I had been there. I can't believe people accept it when other people make those kinds of slurs."

I sighed. "They do, but now we know not everyone agrees with it just because that's what they've heard for years."

"A step in the right direction, for sure. Did this new detective say he was going to be working on Henry's murder?"

"Oh yes, and now that Mary is out of dispatch, we'll find out even more. When I left, they were sorting through the evidence."

Chapter Twenty-Three

The next morning at work, a man in a wrinkled shirt who smelled like he needed a shower stood before me. "Excuse me." He held a faded khaki bucket hat in his hands. "Are you Dot Morgan?"

I had been working on a purchase order for much-needed supplies, and I smelled him before I saw him.

"Yes, I'm Dot. How can I help you?"

He fingered the hat, working his fingers around the rim in a circular motion. When he spoke, I noticed he had a missing tooth on the bottom. "Well, miss, you've already helped me. I'm Bubba Jenkins, and I stopped by to tell you thank you. I was told that it was your efforts that got me out of the pokey. Things were looking mighty bleak for me in there. I'm not sure what you did, but I owe you. If you ever need anything, just let old Bubba know. I'll move the moon and stars to get it."

"You're Bubba?" I stood up and moved to shake his hand. "It's nice to meet you. The whole time you were in jail, I knew you didn't do it. I wasn't even sure why, but you're an innocent man."

"I guess that's what they call that woman's intuition stuff. I'm mighty grateful. Just because I have my boat parked there and, well, sometimes I owe people money around here, you know, the police always think if something bad happens, I probably have to do with it."

"Can I ask you something?"

"Sure, anything."

"You have a boat at the marina. Have you ever seen anything fishy out there? Pardon the pun."

"I'm not sure what you mean by fishy, but plenty is going on, if that's what you're saying. The harbor master keeps pretty busy, uh, entertaining, and when that happens, stuff goes on with the boats. The police kept asking me about what happened with young Henry, but I wasn't anywhere near the marina. I was already hiding out."

"Why were you hiding?"

"Because of what happened to Betty Weaver, I was sure they were going to pin that one on me, you know? Everybody with boats at the marina is respectable, but I didn't even buy my boat. It was left to me, along with harbor fees paid for five years. There's been plenty of nights I go out there to hide or sleep when I don't have any money to pay rent. When this thing with the Weaver girl came up, I just knew they'd be comin' for me. That harbor seems like such a serene place, but let me tell you. Stuff is going on, you know?"

Bubba Jenkins knew more about what was happening at the marina than Shep Olmstead. "Were you there the night Betty Weaver was killed?"

"Oh yeah, I was there, but when I got there, my boat was gone. Someone had skedaddled off with it. I was going to sleep there. I don't got much, but there is a comfy bed in the cabin. I got a crick in my neck that night because I ended up sleeping in my car at the city park. The next day, the boat was back, but whoever took it trashed it. There were beer bottles and gum wrappers. And there was something on the front of it. Not sure what that was."

"So, you think it was your boat that was used to kill Betty?"

"It looks like it, but there's no way I'm going to tell the cops that. I might go in as a concerned citizen, but I'll go out a lifer." He turned the bucket hat in his hands, fingering the rim.

Bubba Jenkins looked bad, smelled bad, but deep down, seemed to be a decent man. "I understand why you were hiding out, then."

"Yes, and well, with that Bailey fella, I thought my number was up. He called you all kinds of names that, frankly, I don't choose to share in mixed company, but I didn't believe a word of it. Now that I've met you, you're just as sweet and kind as Sandra Dee."

"Thanks, Bubba. And thanks for telling me all this. Whoever killed Betty is still out there."

"I know, and I think you're just the gal to get to the bottom of it. Again, I just wanted to say thank you. Not many people stick up for old Bubba in this town." He gave a little bow and backed out of the funeral home.

After Bubba left, I knew his boat connected two deaths. Betty and Henry had the same killer.

Ellie asked me to get off a little early because she wanted to show me something. We'd had a funeral earlier in the day, so things were quiet—not an unusual thing for a funeral home. I left a little before five and stopped by the bridal shop.

"You made it! I've been so excited all day to show this to you."

Ellie ran into the back room and came out with a hanger covered in a plastic case. She held it up high and then put it on a dress rack that stood by the elevated area for brides to look at their dresses.

"Now, I know this is early days, but once we discussed a little about your dress, I took a trial run at it." She unzipped the case and pulled out a bridal gown. It wasn't just any bridal gown, but one of the shortest gowns I'd ever seen. Twiggy would have fit right into that dress, skipping up and down the streets of London. I wasn't as sure that I could pull it off on the streets of Camden.

"Oh my. It's...short."

Ellie puckered her lips. "You said you wanted it mod. I seldom get to sew a dress like this. There's so little to it. I whipped it up in a night. I wish all my wedding dresses were that easy." She took it off the rack and propelled it toward me. "Go ahead, try it on. I'm dying to see it."

I took it reluctantly. Had she only said something besides dying? This wasn't something you said to a person who had been called The Curse of Camden.

Ellie pushed me toward the changing room, and I obediently slipped into the dress. Once on, I looked at myself in the mirror. The dress fit perfectly. There wasn't an inch to spare, but it felt like nothing I'd ever worn before. The silk caressed my skin, and the height of the skirt showcased my upper thighs. I thought about adding white boots and carrying a bouquet of white daisies. I held my hand to my mouth, amazed at the dress my cousin had whipped up.

"Well? Are you going to come out, or do I have to come in there? Don't think I won't," Ellie threatened. After being roommates, I knew she would. Taking a deep breath, I stepped out into the store.

"Wowser," Al said from the curtained doorway that led to the backroom. "You look like something out of one of Ellie's magazines. A dress like that will set Camden on its ear."

"What dress?" Another male voice spoke from behind the curtain. Out stepped Mr. Miller, the janitor from the high school.

"That's a wedding dress? When did brides start wearing only the top half? If my wife had worn that, we would have had to speed up the reception, if you know what I mean."

I felt the heat rising up my neck and spreading to my cheeks. What was the janitor from the school doing in Ellie's back room, holding a wrench?

"Hello, Mr. Miller. This is a surprise."

He gave an abrupt nod. "I'm here for the toilet. Al called me. I have a gift for blocked pipes."

"Sorry, Dot," Ellie said. "But now that the peanut gallery has commented on the dress, I have to tell you, it is stunning on you. If you don't like it, I'll be devastated. Would you mind if I took your picture for future reference?"

"Sure, I guess."

"Great." Ellie pulled a Kodak 110 camera out of the drawer and, after attaching a square flashcube, took a picture, wound the film, and took another. "I never know if I have it the first time. Okay, now, what else should we add to the dress? Any ideas? You knocked it out of the park with the mini-wedding gown."

I stepped up on the bridal stage and looked in the mirror. Ellie rustled to a rack full of tulle and then joined me, placing a veil on the back of my head. Who was that girl in the mirror? Could it be me?

My heart started beating against my chest. I felt like Dorothy, finding the beware, turn back signs on the edge of the Wicked Witch's haunted forest. This was happening. Even though I had a curse hanging over my head, real or unreal, I was getting married. "I think I'm going to need some time. The dress just made the whole wedding planning thing real. I'm in shock."

Ellie hugged my shoulder. "Of course you are. Little Dot is going down the aisle. It's earth-shattering. I know I was a basket case."

"I'll second that," Al said from the doorway.

"The toilet's fixed. I'll go pack up my tools." Mr. Miller let out a low wolf whistle. "Wait till I tell the Mrs. about that dress."

I stepped off the platform. "Um, I was wondering if I could ask you a couple of questions before you go."

Mr. Miller pointed to himself. "Me? I don't know anything about wedding dresses. You're barking up the wrong tree. Now ask me about toilets, and I'm your man."

This guy was funny. I spent four years going through high school and had never spoken to him, other than an occasional "Good morning." Like Bubba, it amazed me how much more there was to people than the way they looked or the job they did. "No, I'm okay with the wedding dress. I wanted to know what you think of Chad Doggett after working with him at the school."

His face hardened. "Normally, I would not express an opinion about a youngin like that, but that kid is worthless. I have the greatest respect for Margaret, but she raised a mess. I'm glad he's leaving town, so I don't have to go behind him and finish the work he didn't do."

It was a comfort to know I wasn't the only one who disliked Chad. "I'm only asking because I think he might have been involved in the deaths of Betty Weaver and Henry Fielding. I know you only worked with him for a brief time, but do you think he might be capable of stealing a boat?"

Mr. Miller looked at Al and then back at me. "I do. He can steal anything on wheels. I say this because he helped me break into my car once. I locked the car and then stupidly lost the keys. I still don't know where I laid them down. Anyhow, he helped me break in with a hanger, and then he reached under the steering column and pulled out some wires. Next thing I knew, the car was running."

"That's something," Al said.

"Sure is," Ellie agreed.

"I'm guessing that with his daddy being Big Buck of Big Buck's Ford, he learned a thing or two about hot-wiring cars. I'll bet he knows how to turn back a speedometer, too. I would guess that's how he learned it."

So, Chad had the skills to start a boat without a key. I had to tell Mary. The police would want to know about this.

"You've been very helpful, Mr. Miller, and you can bet I'm going to take what you said to the police."

His eyes widened. "Now, wait a minute there, Missy." He held up the flat of his palm. "You can't do that."

"Why ever not? I think he might have killed two people."

"Maybe he did, but I'm no snitch. I've spent some time in the county jail, got a little too liquored up at my sister's wedding, and I don't want to get my name out there for getting a guy arrested."

"But I think he did it."

"The school doesn't know about my time behind bars, but if they did, I'd lose my job. I'm not that guy anymore, and I'm happy being a janitor. If you tell the police, you can bet Chad will already know about it."

I understood what he was saying—not wanting to lose his freedom—and I feared he would tell Chad or his mother, Margaret, before I could get to Mary.

Mr. Miller picked up his toolbox. "It sounds like you have a notion about Chad, but don't have any actual proof. Until you do, keep my name out of this. You need to think about what it could do to me."

"I don't have to use your name."

"It'll come up, I guarantee you. Promise me."

I didn't want to, but I agreed with him. "Fine. I'll hold off."

I had to keep what I had learned about Chad's ability to hot-wire a car to myself. He was right. I was close, but I needed more.

When I returned to the funeral home, Neva informed me the florist we used out on the country road still didn't have the van fixed. "We'll need you to drive out and pick up the mums and hydrangeas for the Thompson funeral and be quick about it. This will run us dangerously close to the visitation."

It was a pleasant day, and I didn't mind the drive. Texas put on a show of color in the spring, from the vibrant green of the grass to the brightly colored wildflowers of purple, orange, pink, and yellow. It gave me a few minutes to think things through. I had to get the police after Chad before he could leave town. Even though there were police departments in Dallas, how did we know the two boys would be there? They could go anywhere, and if it was out of state, they could disappear.

Once I picked up the flowers, I propped them up in the back of my car, hoping they wouldn't fall over. Often, the hydrangeas had a little extra water in them, and I'd already had one tip and left a mess on another emergency run for flowers. I had been in the florist shop for a little longer than I planned because Mrs. Simons liked to talk and wanted to hear about my upcoming wedding. She promised that when I was ready to talk about flowers, we would pick out the right ones. When I mentioned daisies, she started listing off the many varieties we could use. She also assured me it was an economical flower to use because weddings were so expensive. As I left the shop, I wondered if every conversation in the next six months would be about my upcoming wedding. I hoped not, because each time I thought about it, I would get a rush of anxiety from feeling overwhelmed.

I checked my Timex and had about a half hour to get back to the funeral home and set up the flowers for the visitation. Luckily, this far out of town, there was little traffic, so I could make good time.

About half a mile down the road, I felt the car swerve, and then, on the driver's side, the front tire beat out a rhythmic tapping on the pavement. I had a flat. I pulled over and jumped out. It wasn't just a little flat, but the wheel itself had become misshapen. The air in it released fast, and upon further examination, my hand ran along a four-inch slit. This wasn't running over a nail. Someone slashed my tire. There had been no one else in the parking lot of the flower shop, but it must have happened when Mrs. Simons distracted me.

"Damn," I said, kicking the tire, causing a hollow thump.

I would have to either walk back to the flower shop or walk into town. Either way, I was wearing heels, and the distance was about the same. I was relieved when a car came up the road and then pulled over behind my car.

"Got a flat?" Chad Doggett got out of his car with a ready smile, a little too wide for the situation. "Isn't that something? Now I'm the one giving advice on your car. What a shame about that tire. It seems like you have a nose for trouble now, don't you?"

"I'm fine." I pulled my arms across my waist. The faster he left, the better off I would be.

"I don't think you are—fine, that is. I think you're a major problem. Thanks to you, the police have been asking me all kinds of questions."

He walked closer and, for the first time, I realized how tall he was. Jeff was taller, but next to me, he felt like a giant. "You're out of luck, though. The cops can't figure it out. Not very smart over there."

His breath lingered under my nose. Beer, and a lot of it.

"You stole Bubba Jenkins's boat, didn't you?"

He shrugged his shoulders. "So? Bubba's such an idiot. He didn't even realize we'd been doing it for months. What business is it of yours?"

"Did you kill Henry? Did you kill him because he might tell everyone that he enlisted in the Army under your name?"

"No." His response was quick and reminded me of a belligerent teenager. "I had nothing to do with Nimrod's death. Yeah, we stole the boat, but I passed out. He was there, but we never killed him. I was too drunk to kill anyone. He was on the boat, fine. Why he got in the water, I don't know." He reached down and grabbed me by the collar of my dress, then pulled my body up so my face was next to his stinking breath. "You need to listen like Henry never could. Stay out of my business, or you'll be sorry. I'll be out of this rathole of a town, and you'll never see me again. Mess with me, and bad things could happen." Chad pushed me back hard, and I landed on the pavement. As he walked away, he pointed at 'y tire. "Too bad. It looks like you have a flat. I hope you like walking." He returned to his car, gunned the motor, and sent gravel flying my way. I folded up my body into the fetal position to avoid getting hit by the spray of rocks. Even though my hands were shaking, and I felt nauseated, I picked myself up, grabbed my purse, and started walking. Keeping Mr. Miller's identity secret was becoming harder to do.

Chapter Twenty-Four

O nce I reached Camden, I stepped into the ice cream parlor and made two calls. One was to Oliver to explain what happened to my car. Neva, very unhappy with me, sent Peter out to get the flowers for the visitation, and even though Oliver offered to help with the tire, I called Ben. It was funny, but there was a transition happening in my life. A couple of years ago, I would have called my parents, but I didn't think twice about calling Ben.

Ben hurried from the paper and picked me up while I was eating a chocolate cone, light on the sprinkles.

"At least you found the upside in all this," he said.

"Yeah, well, in every cloud, there's a silver lining."

He pulled me close, took a lick of my cone, and kissed me, the sweetness still on his lips. "I called a tow truck, and they'll bring your car into the garage. Did you run over a nail?"

Everything Chad said and did was still coursing through me. If I told Ben, he would get angry and go after him. I didn't want Ben anywhere near him. If I were cursed, this would be where my luck would run out. Chad could be a killer, and there was no way I was letting the man I loved anywhere near him. "Those tires are pretty old. I think it might have split in half."

Ben nodded. "After we're married, I'll keep an eye on things like that." I smiled and offered my cone, which he took another lick at.

Ben wanted to go to the garage to arrange for a tow, and I begged off, telling him I wanted to stop in at Blue Bonnets. It was a teeny-weeny little white lie.

I knew what I had to do, and I had to do it by myself. If I got Ben or Mary involved, then something could happen to them. If any harm came, let it come to me. I needed to borrow a car from someone who wouldn't know enough to tell my concerned family. I asked Ben to drop me off at the funeral home, where Peter was unloading the flowers he had retrieved from my car on the country road. As he loaded the flowers in his arms, I had to admit his 1959 Chevy Impala in sleek black, looked like the perfect car for an up-and-coming mortician.

"They're a little wilted, but we can put them out during the visitation. That ought to make things all right with the people who sent them," Peter said as he toted a large display of sad-looking mums. I put my bag down at my desk and helped to carry flowers in. The funeral home was full of mourners, and when Neva saw me, she made a quick motion for me to fix a strand of hair that had fallen during the exhausting walk into town. I placed my flowers in the visitation room and ran back to my desk to get my bag. I quickly pulled out my compact, restored my hair, and put on lipstick.

Peter passed me, carrying another load of flowers. "You look great. Don't worry about it."

With a smile, I set aside my makeup and relieved Peter of a pot filled with drooping geraniums. "Thanks. Could I ask you a little favor?"

"Sure. Anything," Peter answered as he led the way back into the visitation room.

"Could I borrow your car for a couple of hours tonight?"

He turned slightly. "I guess so." His willingness to do this so quickly made me wonder if he was a nice guy or had a little crush on me. I hoped he was just a nice guy.

"Thank you. I promise I'll bring it right back. No dents. No scratches."

"Okay." He looked unsure of my promises. "Just for tonight."

We placed the final two pots in the visitation room and then walked out. When we were almost out of earshot, he whispered, "Can I ask what you're using it for?"

I hadn't counted on that question, and I had never been a good liar. I went with a half-truth. "It's nothing, really. I was going to...um...meet someone out at the marina."

He raised his eyebrows. "Really? Why the marina? I mean, I know I'm new to town and everything, but isn't that the thing that's been connected to these murders?"

"Is it?" It sounded like a lie the minute I said it.

Suddenly, Peter raised his head as a thought hit him. "I know what this is about. You're going with your reporter boyfriend to spy on the marina. Track down a killer. Is that it?"

Wow. I didn't know Peter had paid this much attention to my comings and goings. "Why would you say that?"

"Come on, Dot. You're a legend around here. You get involved with murders, and then you solve them."

I blushed. It was nice to be called a legend and not a curse for once.

"You're famous. So, you and your boyfriend are on the case, I guess."

"Yes. On the case." It sounded like I was Eliot Ness from the TV show *The Untouchables* when he put it that way.

"Well," I heard him jingling the keys in his pocket. "Is this dangerous? I mean, do I need to tell someone like your friend, Mary, the cop?"

Once again, I was amazed at what Peter knew about me. I also did not want to involve Mary, at least not yet. I knew I was being silly, but I had this overwhelming feeling of dread. I would not let the curse strike anyone I loved. No. I could think my way through this. "No! Don't be silly. I'll be fine."

"Don't you mean the two of you will be fine?"

I had forgotten to include Ben. "Right. We'll be fine." I stressed "we'll" to make sure my lie sounded convincing. I was better at lying than I thought.

"Okay, but maybe having the police know what you're doing might be the prudent thing to do."

This kid was wearing me out. "No need to bother the police. This is just a stakeout. You know, like the detectives on TV."

"Cool. If you'll drop me at my house, you can borrow my car," he paused, "but only if you tell me all about it tomorrow."

"You bet," I said, hoping he wouldn't hold me to it.

Chapter Twenty-Five

I had never felt so alone as I did in this moment. I also felt a little foolish that night, shivering behind the wheel of Peter's car as I waited. This time, when I lied to Ben, it came easier than trying to convince Peter to borrow his car. I told him that I was exhausted from walking into town and would go to bed early. He accepted it easily, which made me feel guilty. I would explain it all to him later and could only hope he would understand.

I was counting on a couple of things. One, if I lost control of the situation, maybe Shep Olmstead would hear my blood-curdling screams from his house. Second, maybe, and this was a big maybe, Jeff seemed like a guy who could listen to reason if presented with enough facts. I hoped he would listen to what I had to say and help me with Chad. It was a little before eight, and I was strongly doubting the logic of the plan I had devised while sitting in the ice cream parlor waiting for Ben. If he knew, he'd be furious. But if I was going to protect him from the curse, I needed to keep him away. I would take care of him the way he promised to take care of me, whether it was a flat tire or something else. That was what marriage was all about, or at least that's what ours would be like. If I would beat this curse thing, I had to be proactive, and that was what I was doing.

The wind came up, and the boats rocked against the edge of the dock. It was peaceful out here, and there was no jazz coming from Shep Olmstead's house tonight. His afternoon liaison must have been at her PTA meeting or with her husband and children. It was amazing what you could find out in a small town by listening and watching. People held secrets behind their perfect little white houses. Marigolds planted out front, freshly painted white gingerbread architecture, a homey atmosphere on the outside, but secrets inside the world would amaze at. Some secrets came out, and some went to the graveyard with them.

The same car that pulled up behind me in the country pulled into the parking lot of the marina. Chad got out of the driver's seat, and Jeff came out on the passenger side. When the two boys were apart, they seemed less of a threat. Together, it was as if they grew strength from each other and the rest of the world be damned.

I left the comfort and security of Peter's car and walked over to where the two stood.

"You wanted to see us?" Chad asked, a lewd look in his eye. "I know it's hard for a chick like you to resist my charms, right?"

Jeff laughed. "Be serious, Chad. That's not what she's here for. She has a boyfriend. No. The Curse of Camden is out to solve another murder. Did you like the article in the paper? I'm sure that'll slow you down next time you go whining to the cops."

Why hadn't I thought of that? They were the ones to plant the article in the paper. Who else had a motive to do that? "Did you put that in the paper? Was it you?"

Jeff rolled his head back and laughed, catching Chad's eye. Chad responded with his own laugh, which made Jeff smile even more. When he talked, he spoke in a whiny voice. "Why would you say that? I have nothing but respect for you, Dot, the homecoming queen. Oh, baby, you're my dream come true."

They both started laughing, and I felt a little of what Henry must have had to endure every day of high school. Jeff pulled out a pack of gum, unwrapped a piece and stuck it in his mouth. He threw the gum wrapper to the ground. I needed to shut them up, and I knew how.

I blurted out my words, effectively quieting them. "I know you killed them, Chad. Both of them. Betty and Henry."

That did it. They stopped like a needle ripped off a record. "You don't know anything," Jeff said.

"Yes, actually, I do. I know you had Bubba Jenkins's boat out, and on the night Henry died, he was with you. You killed him. I'm not exactly sure why, but I would guess it might be because he was going to tell your father he faked your enlistment. Was that it? Did he want more money, or sadly, your friendship? You have no idea what your bullying did to Henry. He never stopped wanting to have you as a friend, although I couldn't tell you why anyone would want that."

Chad stepped forward, and I stepped back. "I told you already that I was passed out drunk. I had nothing to do with Henry Fielding's death."

"How am I supposed to believe that?"

Chad's eyes widened. "How many times do I have to tell you this? Whatever happened to Henry, we had no part in it." He turned to Jeff. "Right Jeff? Tell her?"

When Jeff didn't answer right away, Chad repeated his words this time with an underlying tone of menace. "Tell her."

Jeff's eyes grew cold and then they turned on m. "You're a problem, Dot Morgan. A much bigger one than I had considered. I misjudged you. It's a shame to have to kill such a perfect specimen of femininity."

"Jeff? What are you talking about?" Chad looked confused.

"Don't worry about it. Dot's a problem, and I'm going to make sure she doesn't bother us anymore."

Chad looked confused at his friend's words. "And how are you going to do that? What are you going to do? Kill her?"

It was in that moment I realized I had misjudged the dynamics between Chad and Jeff. I assumed Chad was the leader, mostly because Jeff followed along in everything he did, but there was something more here. Much more. I snapped my fingers. "Of course. Chad wasn't the only one there, but I'm confused about a motive. Killing another human being requires a deep anger." I focused my gaze on Jeff. I had been wrong all along. "Why did you kill Henry, Jeff?"

"I didn't kill anybody." His low tone was soft, but the menace was there.

I tried to keep the shakes out of my own voice. "You did. I didn't see it at first, but you most definitely did."

Chad stumbled backward. "Jeff? You told me it was an accident. That you were telling him to get off the front of the boat, but he couldn't hear you.

You were going too fast, and he flew off and hit his head on a rock. That isn't what happened?"

Jeff's eyes were empty as he stared at me. There was no remorse, no fear, nothing. Then he switched his gaze to Chad, and with that, everything changed. He became flustered. "Didn't I fix it with Betty? I didn't tell anyone about how drunk you were when you hit her, and no one ever suspected you, especially when we showed up at the funeral. It was an accident, but the cops would never see it that way. I had to save you. I fixed it for you, and now I'm going to fix this."

So much was being said, I had to ask again. "So, you killed Henry? You killed him for Chad?"

"Yes, and I'm going to do it again." Jeff's tone was deliberate, yet distant. To him, I was a minor problem, like a speck of dust on his shoe. He didn't feel the terror he was causing in me as my heart raced and my mind desperately tried to come up with an escape plan through the panic. I was simply a means to an end.

Chad was still stuck on the thought of his friend killing someone on purpose. "You killed Henry? The deaf kid? Why would you do that? I could have handled him."

What had driven Jeff to kill someone as sweet as Henry? "Yes, Jeff, why did you have to go to the extreme of killing Henry Fielding? Why?"

Jeff's face began to redden, and then he shrieked at me like a banshee on a winter night. "Because he was hurting Chad and me." His face looked contorted in the moonlight. He was no longer the smiling vacuum cleaner salesman, but the person he really was. Someone feeling a strong passion. Something in my brain clicked, and it became clear. It was the thing my dad had made a point of not to talk about at his birthday party. "You're in love with Chad, aren't you?"

"What?" Chad yelled with an edge of disgust in his voice. "What are you talking about? Don't say things like that."

And with that, I knew I'd struck a nerve in Chad, proving this relationship was one way and one way only. He did not know the true nature of his friend's devotion, and I had to make it clear to him. "Jeff can't bear to be away from you and will do anything to keep the two of you together because he's in love with you. Haven't you felt it?"

"No. That's not true." He turned to Jeff. "That's not true, right? You're not—"

"It is true," I interrupted. "He's in love with you, not as a friend, but something more. Think about it. Why is it that he discourages all your girlfriends from staying in your life? He wants you to himself, even if he can't have a romantic relationship with you. People kill for love, Chad, and Jeff killed for you."

For the first time, I saw what looked like deep emotion in Jeff's eyes.

Chad put his hands over his ears. "You're lying. You're just trying to break apart our friendship. Shut up!"

"It was right in front of you, and you never realized it. Look at Jeff and tell me I'm lying." I stopped talking and lowered his hands, his eyes on Jeff, his childhood friend.

"It's true, Chad," Jeff whispered, and then he stared at the ground.

Chad doubled over. "Oh, my God. Oh, my God."

"I couldn't tell you. I could never tell you." As he spoke, tears worked their way into Jeff's words.

There was so much pain between them I felt sad for both of them. Jeff could never express the love he felt for his friend, and Chad could never accept it.

Suddenly, Jeff was in front of me, grabbed me by the back of my neck, pushed me over to the edge of the dock, and rammed my head into the water. I kicked and tried to scream, but the algae-filled lake started filling my lungs. This was it. The curse had finally come for me.

I reached back and elbowed him in the gut, escaping into the dark waters of the marina. He jumped in after me and latched onto my neck once more, dunking my head under the water. I fought with all my might, reaching not for the hand pushing me down, but to Jeff's leg. I pulled hard and heard him splash into the water next to me, his grip lessening enough I could pull away.

I swam under the dark water, hoping he could not see me, but with this escape, there was another danger. I couldn't see the boats parked in the marina well. In the murky water, they were nothing more than blurry outlines. I had to get out into the harbor, away from Jeff. I swam as fast as I could, bumping against the edge of the dock. It hurt my shoulder, but it also told me I was about to be out in the open space of the lake. I had to keep swimming faster and faster even though my chest was aching from the exertion.

If I could make it to the shore further down, I could run into the woods and away from Jeff. I kept pushing my arms through the water when suddenly, my leg caught on something. I pulled up out of the water. Jeff was holding onto my ankle and was attempting to get closer to me. He pulled my leg to his side, bringing my body up next to his. Dropping my leg, he transferred his grip to my shoulders, pushing me down into the blackness. I tried hitting his midsection, making his body bound backward, but it wasn't enough to stop him. I was about to land one between his legs when the pressure on my shoulders lifted.

I rose out of the water and realized Chad had joined us. Jeff was no longer trying to kill me, but battling Chad. They wrestled in the water as Chad tried to push his lifelong friend under the water. "I am not like that. They'll think I'm like that."

I started swimming back to the dock to get away from them. If Jeff could get away from Chad, he would come after me. It amazed me that Chad was more concerned with what the town would think of as a homosexual affair than a murder. It was the whole reason Jeff never revealed his true feelings. There was too much at stake, and he knew it. How many times had Chad made jokes about people like him, and he was forced to laugh along? I pulled myself up on the dock, ran to Shep's house, and banged on the door. Within a minute, he came out blurry-eyed, tying the belt of a ratty blue robe.

"What?" He yelled as he opened the door.

"Call the police. Chad Doggett is trying to kill Jeff Hudson, who was trying to kill me."

He ran a hand through his thinning hair. "Christ on a cracker." He turned to make the call, and I went back out. They were still splashing, trying to get the edge on the other.

"I hate you! How could you?" Chad screamed. That was when I noticed. There was no longer any noise coming from Jeff. Chad had killed him, either by drowning him or strangling him. I couldn't be sure. However he did it, it was done, and now he was raging at Jeff's lifeless body.

When the police pulled up, Chad was sitting on the dock with one of Shep's towels around his shoulders. He hadn't even bothered to run. Jeff lay out on the dock, dead.

Mary put her arm around me. "You crazy woman. Why didn't you tell me you were going to confront a killer? I know you got this wedding thing on your brain, but this was not only loco, but it was also damn dangerous."

"I know. I know."

"Thank God you're all right."

After nearly being killed and having to think in a crisis, I felt myself calming down. Once I did that, the tears flowed, and I sobbed into Mary's shoulder. Even though I had confronted two murderers who acted like the lives they took were not important, somehow, I felt sorry for them.

Chapter Twenty-Six

Ben paced the room. "So, you decided, all by yourself, that you would face off with two killers because of what?"

I drew out a sigh and rubbed the back of my neck. It was still sore where Jeff had held me under the water. "I was protecting you."

Ben looked incredulous. "You were protecting me? From two big guys with a track record of murdering people."

We were in the lobby of the police station, waiting to be dismissed by Detective Barrera, and I felt exhaustion creeping in. I just wanted to go home and crawl into bed, and I only hoped that when I shut my eyes, I wouldn't dream about not being able to breathe in the murky water. I wasn't doing a very good job of explaining this to him, and why would he understand, anyway? A curse? That's for gypsies and witches. No one believes in curses anymore.

"Please, Ben. I'm sorry, but I had to."

The tears came back again, which didn't look good when my parents came running in the door with Ellie and Al behind them. My mother grabbed me, and then my dad grabbed us both.

"Thank God you're all right, Dot," my dad whispered into my hair. "I don't know how you get yourself into these messes, but I guess you're blessed because you always come out of them whole and hearty."

Blessed. He said I was blessed. He was right. I was incredibly blessed. I just faced off with two men who had killed and survived it. This is not what happens to a person who is cursed. This happens to someone who has good things happening to them. Blessed. In that moment, he made my fears of hurting the ones I loved go away in a puff of smoke.

"I love you, Dad."

Making a grown man cry in front of his future son-in-law was something I shouldn't have done, but what can I say? He was always the one crying into the popcorn at the movies. How could you not love that?

"I love you too, Pumpkin," he responded.

My parents pulled away, and Ellie hugged me, with Al standing back. He made a quiet comment that I don't think he intended for anyone to hear. "Yep. Better than Peyton Place, our Miss Dot is."

Ellie pushed at his shoulder and then focused on me. "I guess your curse has been removed now."

"Why would you say that?" I asked, hope in my voice.

"Because you got into one of your messes, and we're all fine. Isn't that what you told me? You were afraid something would happen to Ben?" She looked over at Ben, who, at that moment, had a confused expression on his face.

Recognition hit Ben's features. He tilted his head forward, his hands in his pockets. He was astonished at this news. "You thought I would die? You were protecting me? You thought I would be the next victim of the Camden Curse?"

I bit my bottom lip. "Yes."

He let out a little snort. "Is that why you wouldn't set a date for so long?"

I nodded.

"Oh, Dot, my Dot." He took my hand. "I thought you were having second thoughts about me. Do you know what that can do to a man? I'd been blaming myself all along and I wasn't the problem, you were."

When he put it that way, I laughed. All the thoughts that had been going through my head, repeating themselves. Most of it was manufactured by me. I was my own worst enemy.

Ben took my hand and looked into my eyes. "Don't you realize that when we're together, nothing bad can happen to either of us? We'll work our way out of whatever bumps we hit."

"That's what love is all about," Al echoed him with his flat Texas twang.

"Okay, stop everybody before we break out into song," I said, and we did break out into laughter.

Detective Barrerra came in and smiled. "I have to say, you people don't act like the normal crowd."

He turned to me. "You, young lady, take way too many chances. I don't know what you were thinking, meeting up with two people you were sure were murderers…alone…without telling anybody. I swear, sometimes it feels like one of those B movies. Still, we have a confession. Chad had no idea how his buddy felt about him, and when he found out, he couldn't handle it."

"Unrequited love is a messy thing," my mother said.

"Yes, well, this is the first time I've seen it lead to murder. We'll be gathering the facts in the coming days just to lock the case down. I need to interview the marina owner, what's his name? Olmstead? He seems to be hard to catch, especially in the afternoons." Barrerra looked genuinely perplexed while Ben and I exchanged glances.

"I'm just glad you didn't send an innocent man to jail," I said.

"Yes, about that. Detective Bailey is no longer with the department. He did not take too kindly to having a partner. I guess he's always worked solo."

Mary muttered under her breath. "Probably because no one could stand him."

If Barrerra heard it, he didn't respond. "You can all go home, although, last I checked, I was only holding one witness. I'm not quite sure how this many people ended up in here."

Mary smiled. "That's the way it is around here. Friends and family barge in whenever they're needed."

I reached out and pulled Mary into a hug. "And thank God, they do."

Chapter Twenty-Seven

Oliver sat in his office chair as I explained the circumstances that led to Henry's death.

"It all seems like my son was expendable to them. A boy I spent my life loving and raising, and to them, he was a minor problem to take care of. That was it. Now I'm hearing this had to do with what was going on between them. My son had to die for this?"

"I'm sorry. I know it's painful."

"Don't be sorry. It's hard to hear, but I needed to know. Henry's death is all I have left of Henry's life, you know?"

There was a knock at the door of Oliver's office. When I turned around from where I was sitting, Dina White stood there, her eyes on Oliver. "I came as soon as I could. Everyone in town is talking about what happened at the marina and what it had to do with Henry. Are you all right, Oliver?"

Oliver rose from the desk and quickly made his way to her arms. She hugged him and then, when they parted slightly, reached up and pushed a piece of hair off his forehead. "It's okay now. Now we know."

Oliver buried his head in her shoulder. Neva walked in on the scene and cleared her throat.

"Oliver?" she asked, not looking too pleased at the display of affection going on in front of her. Oliver pulled away. "Mother, Dot here just explained everything that happened at the marina. It's a lot."

"Yes, I'm sure it is. I just got off the phone with Mrs. Simons from the florist shop, and she couldn't wait to tell me about it," she turned toward me, "and thank you, Dot, for letting Oliver know." Her gaze shifted to Dina. "And thank you, Mrs. White, for being such a good friend to Oliver."

Dina straightened her jacket as she pulled away from Oliver's embrace. "Of course. I'd do anything for Oliver."

"That's very sweet of you. Having a friend at a time like this is vital. You have been a rock for my son."

"Mother," Oliver said. "Dina and I are more than friends."

Neva looked confused. "What do you mean?"

"After Henry's death, I realized some things in my life. Mistakes. One thing was, it is important to love the people around you when they are still alive. Dina and I have been dancing around our feelings for each other for years. After Henry, I realized I needed more. I reached out, and she was there."

"Just what exactly are you saying, Oliver?" Neva not only looked confused, but a little irritated.

"He's saying," Dina answered. "Oliver and I are in love. We've decided to get married."

Neva's face went white, slightly resembling some of her clientele. "You're getting married? So soon after Henry's death? Are you sure this is a good idea? When did all this happen? Honestly, Oliver, you've never even gone through a proper engagement."

"No," Oliver said. "And we've never officially been seen as a couple, but we were. We were always together at the boys' events. We did everything together as if we had been a family, just not in the legal sense. Nelson knows, and he's happy for us, although he told me he wishes Henry were here to share in our happiness."

"I see. Well, this is a lot to take in, son. Are you sure that this whole 'thing' with this woman isn't a result of the emptiness of losing Henry? You may wake up in a year and realize you were simply trying to quell your loneliness. You will realize that everything you were looking for you already had. A good family and the responsibility of running your father's business. Trust me. A year from now, you might be rethinking this rash decision to marry." She turned to Dina. "What do you know about living with someone who works in a funeral home?"

"Like Oliver said, we've been side by side for years. I know because I've

170

been here, Neva. I'm guessing you didn't notice."

"I don't know. I wish your father were here to guide me. I'm not sure how this will affect Fielding Funeral Home."

Oliver took Dina's hand. "And is that what your major concern is in all of this?"

"Of course it is. Your father left me here to make sure Fielding Funeral Home continues. Now, with you gallivanting off to get married, it makes me unsure of what will happen next."

Oliver put his hand to his chin. "Mother, you amaze me sometimes. Most mothers would have said, 'Congratulations, son. I'm glad you're happy after all that's happened.' Yet, your primary concern is about the bottom line here at the funeral home?"

"Someone has to be the grownup. It's my job."

"No, your job is to be my mother first. Everything else is not important. You want to know what I think about this funeral home? I think there are some days I feel like I'm being smothered. I worked every day to make sure that I helped you carry on Father's wishes, but nothing was ever as good as when he was running the place. Nothing. Now that Henry is gone, I really don't enjoy being here."

"How can you say that? This is our family business. It's like an extension of our home."

"It's an extension of *your* home mother, not mine."

Neva started nodding her head back and forth quickly. "You're over-wrought and think you've found some strange form of happiness with Mrs. White. I'm going to leave you so you can pull yourself together, and then we can talk about this later."

"No."

Neva straightened her spine. "No?"

"No." Oliver's answer was short and to the point. "Dina and I have been talking and have decided it would be better for us to start anew. Nelson wants to attend college in San Antonio, and there is a funeral home for sale over there."

"You have to be joking. You would leave Fielding Funeral Home? What about me? Am I supposed to run this business on my own?"

"I didn't say that. Mother, how old are you? Honestly?"

Neva put her hand on the folds of her neck. "You know how old I am. 81."

"Exactly. You are at an age when ladies retire. Why haven't you retired? I know you're tired. I see it all the time, but it's like this madness you have inside of you."

"That's silly."

I, too, remembered the days when Neva would leave to put her feet up and rest. I knew no one else her age who worked as much as she did.

"Is it? I think you're afraid if you quit working here, you'll lose your memory of my father."

"How can you say that? You're against me. You're all against me," Neva said as she bustled down the hall.

Oliver ran after her. Twenty minutes later, he returned, hands in his pockets. "She's okay. She's accepted it, although she's not happy."

Dina put her arm through his. "This was rough for her. First, you're getting married and then you told her she was too old for the job. Not exactly easy to hear."

"Yes," he said softly, "but it was something she needed to hear, don't you agree?"

"Are you sure about this?" I asked, leaning up against a dark cherry credenza where Oliver kept his forms.

"Yes. I had always intended to pass the business down to Henry, but now that won't be possible." Oliver stood and looked out the window. The spring blossoms were coming in, and pink showed from the crepe myrtle tree planted near the glass. "When a child is lost, you learn of the people who loved them and never told you. Not the same kind of love, but love. Dina and her boys have always been a part of our lives. When we lost Henry, I realized that even though we never dated, we needed each other. In our way, the four of us had become a family over the years. I felt so alone, but then Dana was there. Something between us changed. My mother was right in that was probably my attempt to fill the gaping hole left by Henry's death, but now it's comfortable, our being together. It gives me the strength to move on with my life. You can understand that, can't you?"

"Sure. I'm happy for you, Oliver." And I was. He went through so much pain after Henry died. Anything that made him happy, have hope, be willing to get up the next day, was a wonderful thing.

"You should know, Peter has made an offer on the funeral home. His parents are the actual buyers, but we are closing the deal. The thing is, he doesn't need a receptionist. His mother will do that duty and many more, I guess. I hate to tell you this, but I'll have to let you go."

I should have seen this coming. The thought of applying for more jobs filled me with discouragement. I was becoming a pariah in the workforce.

"Okay."

"I'm sorry."

"It can't be helped." And that was exactly what I told Ben that night.

"It will be okay. You'll find another job."

"Who is left in this town to hire me? It's bad enough I've been involved in a murder…"

"A couple of murders."

"A couple of murders, but now I have this legend around me. I'm an albatross, a bad luck charm." I was about to say more, but Ben stopped it with a kiss.

"You are the best thing that has ever happened to this town. You're smart, beautiful," he touched my cheek, "sexy, and about to be my wife. Be happy."

"At least I don't have to run into Chad Doggett anymore."

As the months to the trial neared, Ellie got bigger and bigger, and the date for our wedding neared. It amazed me that Chad never knew Jeff's feelings for him, and when he did, he couldn't handle it. His mother, Margaret, was always there, sitting in the front row behind her son. Chad's father and brother never attended a single day of the trial, not even the sentencing. Margaret always stood by her boy, even when no one else would. If I ever gave birth to a son, would I be so blinded by love I could not see him for who he was? Maybe. Especially if he looked like Ben.

Chad Doggett was charged with murder for killing Jeff and for manslaughter for hitting Betty Weaver while drunk. He was looking at spending most of his life in prison. Here was a young man who had spent so much time trying to be free of life's burdens and now he would never find that freedom. The person he would have confided in over all of it, couldn't even be there to listen. Just the thought of Chad's downfall made me sad.

Bubba Jenkins got his boat back with a few repairs by the marina guy after something about friends helping friends and keeping each other secrets. The wood-paneled station wagon still shows up several times a week, and Billie Holiday is a favorite.

Oliver, Dina, Nelson, and Arnie moved to San Antonio, where Nelson would start college in the fall and Arnie would attend Burnet Elementary School. They had a very quiet wedding at the courthouse, and my father, who works there as a clerk, let me know so I could throw some rice their way. Neva was there as well as Dina's parents. Neva did not look happy about it, but put on a brave face. I ran into Oliver's new family in the early summer when they were out at the park for the Fourth of July. Arnie and Nelson were tossing a football with Oliver, and even though Dina said they were up to their elbows in packing, they seemed to have found a happy place after so much grief.

Fielding Funeral Home has now been renamed the Camden Funeral Home, although I can't tell you much about it. I haven't been back since the day I left when Peter told me he was about to hire a new assistant fresh out of mortuary school.

As I tidied up my desk that day, the familiar routine of packing my things into a sturdy cardboard box felt strangely bittersweet. Memories mingled with office supplies as I carefully organized my belongings, each item carrying its own story of days gone by.

Downstairs, the low murmur of conversation floated up to me, a blend of Peter's enthusiastic voice and the eager tones of the new intern. Their discussion of science provided a curious backdrop to the somber atmosphere of the funeral home, a reminder that life's complexities often intersect in unexpected ways.

Neva's disapproval lingered like a shadow, her discontent palpable in the air. Her parting words, heavy with skepticism, replayed in my mind like a broken record. She had voiced her concerns about Peter's ability to uphold her family's legacy, oblivious to the irony of her own prophecy.

Yet, as I reflected on the past week, a sense of optimism washed over me. Despite Neva's doubts, Peter had proven himself to be a capable leader. His willingness to seek guidance from Oliver demonstrated humility and respect for tradition, qualities that boded well for the future of the funeral home.

As I prepared to bid farewell to this chapter of my life, I couldn't help but feel a twinge of sadness mixed with hope. Change was inevitable, but in Peter's hands, I trusted that the essence of the funeral home would endure, a testament to the resilience of the human spirit and the power of tradition to transcend generations.

As I noticed the drooping lily, I felt a twinge of sympathy. I briefly considered giving it water, but then remembered it was now Peter's responsibility. Imagining Neva's reaction to neglecting it made me chuckle.

Thinking about funeral homes, I realized they were more than just fancy buildings. They held memories of laughter and tears, woven together like a tapestry. Henry's awkward smiles and Oliver's comforting words came to mind, reminding me of the impact this place had on me.

Leaving the funeral home, I couldn't help but think about the lessons I learned there. It wasn't just a job; it taught me empathy and resilience. Even though it might not fit neatly on my resume, I knew those experiences would stay with me as I moved forward.

It was later that summer the town council dedicated a corner of the park to Betty Weaver. Per her wishes, they enclosed an area just for the town's dogs. I went to the ceremony with my parents. Betty's dad was there with a beautiful golden retriever who was allowed to be the first dog to enter the park.

He took the leash off the dog's collar. "Go on in there, Belle. This is your gift from Betty. I just know she's here with us even if she isn't."

The solemn eyes of the golden retriever looked at Mr. Weaver, and then, with a bark that echoed across the park, he ran to the farthest corner of the fencing and then ran back. After that, other dog owners released their dogs one by one. The dogs of all sizes ran and frolicked in their very own park.

Mr. Weaver was right. Betty was there in every tail wag.

Chapter Twenty-Eight

Four Months Later

I t was two weeks before our wedding and Ellie's thin body had ballooned. The due date of her baby had moved up a couple of weeks, so now she was due the last week of August. She never was good at math. After being called The Curse of Camden, I decided to take some time off before looking for work. Actually, arranging my wedding was turning into a full-time job. Between flowers, caterers, venues, and photographers, I was pretty busy. No one had seen my wedding dress but Ellie and Al and I swore them to secrecy. The bigger Ellie got, the more she mourned the loss of her waist as she watched me twirl around in her" Twiggy" wedding dress.

My mother and Aunt Mavis gave Ellie a baby shower, and of course, Mavis gave her a tiny set of combat boots for the new arrival. "You never know when you'll find yourself stuck in the muck," she said, assuring us all we were destined to be knee-deep in mud very soon.

When I wasn't on the phone setting up the wedding, I began to explore other things I could do besides being a secretary. My thoughts revolved around the local college. I wanted to do more than type up dictation and file invoices for other people, but I wasn't sure yet what that would be. Yes, we settled into summer, with Ben back to doing local news and Ellie giving Barbara more responsibility at the shop.

Two days before the wedding, we were waiting for Al to meet us at our future home, a small rental house that was only a little bigger than my apartment. Ben thought it might be a good idea for Al to check out the electrical system, and I agreed adding it might be good to get the plumbing checked as well. This sunny little yellow house was perfect for us. There were two flower beds in front filled with purple and yellow petunias, and a large red oak shaded the front half of the roof. I couldn't wait to move in right after the wedding. After waiting for Al for an hour, I began to worry about Ellie going into premature labor, so I called Bluebonnets.

Ellie was in the middle of a very heavy wedding season, so her words were brief when she answered the phone.

"Bluebonnets."

"Hey, Ellie. Al was supposed to meet us at the rental house. Is everything okay? Do you know where he is?"

"Uh, no. He might be stuck at a job, but he told me this morning he would be meeting the two of you at your new house. He isn't there?"

"No, he's not."

"That's not like him. When he's running late at one appointment, he always uses the phone where he is to call the next appointment."

"Okay, but we don't have a phone here."

"Yes, but I do. He would have called me to get a message to you. Al always lets me know what he's doing." Ellie stopped talking and let out a sound I couldn't be sure of. Was she angry at Al, or was it something else?

"Ellie? Are you all right?"

"Fine."

"Ellie. You sound funny to me. What's going on?"

Ellie didn't speak at first but then said, "I think we need to find Al....now."

That was the beginning of the day that changed everything. I worried Al would miss the birth of his child. My wedding, the focus of my entire summer, no longer seemed as important to me.

Acknowledgements

Thank you to my editor, Shawn at Level Best.

About the Author

Teresa Trent started out teaching English in Colorado, but life and children intervened, and with all that new spare time, she began writing. Besides The Swinging Sixties Series, Teresa has penned the Pecan Bayou, Piney Woods and Henry Park Mystery Series and always has a little idea in the back of her mind for the next one. She is also the author of several short stories and is teaching writing at her local library encouraging new writers. Teresa lives in Houston, Texas with her husband and son.

AUTHOR WEBSITE:
  https://teresatrent.com
  https://teresatrent.blog

SOCIAL MEDIA HANDLES:
  FACEBOOK: https://www.facebook.com/teresatrentmysterywriter
  TWITTER: https://twitter.com/ttrent_cozymys
  BLOG: https://teresatrent.blog/ (Books to the Ceiling)
  WEBSITE: http://teresatrent.com
  GOODREADS: https://www.goodreads.com/author/show/5219581.Teresa_Trent
  INSTAGRAM: https://www.instagram.com/teresatrent_cozymys/
  BOOKBUB: https://www.bookbub.com/profile/teresa-trent

Also by Teresa Trent

The Swinging Sixties Series
The Twist and Shout Murder
If I had a Hammer
Listen, Do You Want to Know a Secret

www.ingramcontent.com/pod-product-compliance
Lightning Source LLC
Chambersburg PA
CBHW020721130726
47899CB00011B/834